Praise for Sandy Lynn's *Kiss and Tell*

"A wonderful blend of romance and paranormal"
~ *Catherine Smith, ParaNormal Romance*

"Kiss and Tell was thoroughly enjoyable. ...The characters were well developed and the sex scenes were hot. Kiss and Tell is book one of a series and I can't wait to sink my teeth into the rest, as I am already addicted..."
~ *Barb, Joyfully Reviewed*

"KISS AND TELL had me laughing and intrigued at the same time. ...Willow is experiencing rapture unlike any other and she takes the readers along for the ride."
~ *Angel, Blue Ribbon Reviews*

"I really like this novel. It is very humorous and hot, and I really like the way that Ms. Lynn brought a lot of originality to the vampire romance. ...Ms. Lynn does a super red-hot job on this book, and I cannot wait to see what she does with the next book in this series."
~ *Missy, Fallen Angel Reviews*

"KISS AND TELL starts out with a bang and the action never stops... With a talented turn of phrase, characters that you'll come to care about, and a pen that writes scorching love scenes, Sandy Lynn has proven herself to be an author to watch out for. Don't miss KISS AND TELL, the first in the BloodMates series from Samhain Publishing."

~ Lori Ann, Romance Reviews Today

Kiss and Tell

Sandy Lynn

A Samhain Publishing, Ltd. publication.

Samhain Publishing, Ltd.
512 Forest Lake Drive
Warner Robins, GA 31093
www.samhainpublishing.com

Editing by Angie James
Cover by Scott Carpenter

First Samhain Publishing, Ltd. electronic publication: February 2007
First Samhain Publishing, Ltd. print publication: January 2008

Dedication

For my friends. I'd like to thank everyone who has supported me through this time in my life and helped to encourage me. For Heather, Ferra, Jess, Kita, Shelly, Joy, Elaine and Sarah. Thanks you guys for being there for me and listening to me whenever I needed to talk. And thank you to anyone I forgot to mention in my list. I don't know what I'd do without you guys!

Chapter One

"Who's up tonight?" Mary asked, scanning the large crowd in the group's favorite bar, The Grunge.

"Willow."

"Nuh-uh, not me. You do it, Roxy. I told you guys, I'm only here to listen to the Night Crawlers. I am not getting involved in your kinky little game." The band's metal beat filled the building, capturing people as the lead singer's mesmerizing voice half-sang and half-shouted the songs. The crowd surged, jumping from the energy of the music.

"Will." Roxy gave an exaggerated sigh. "Sometimes it's hard to remember we're sisters. Come on, you just got fired, have a little fun, get a little wild. Really, would it kill you to just let loose for once?"

"Probably." Looking at her sister, Willow knew Roxy wouldn't stop until she agreed to play this once. "Fine. But only one guy. I mean it."

"Deal." Roxy smiled, pouncing on the victory.

The women each had a drink in front of them as they carefully looked over the crowd. The promise of live music had the bar more crowded than usual. With a little luck

Willow would be able to pick a guy and get this over with so she could go back to fuming about her asshole ex-boss. Each of the trio looked around, searching all the men they could find for a possible target for Willow.

The band is the only reason worth being here tonight, Willow thought sullenly. She continued scanning the crowd for someone to become her prey, but she wasn't having much luck. It seemed almost impossible to find a single man—besides a member of the band—with whom she would be interested in playing her friends' game. She wished she could choose anyone, but she didn't want to have to risk paying a forfeit to just anyone. By playing the game, she ran the chance of having to kiss her target. And she wasn't willing to kiss over half the men she'd seen that night.

As she sat facing the bar's entrance, Willow opened her mouth. She had every intention of promising to take her single "turn" another night and going home. Not even the music from her favorite band seemed to soothe the sting from her earlier meeting with her former boss. Instead of speaking, her lips curved into a smile as two huge biker types walked in, pushing their way through the crowd.

As she watched, she had to correct her thoughts. The first man didn't walk. He strode through the place as though he owned it, completely at ease with everything around him. Willow felt her interest stirring immediately and sat a little straighter in her chair. He was exactly the type of man she would love to kiss. Hell, he was the kind of man she would love to do even more with.

He looked tall—over six feet if she had to guess—with warm brown hair hanging just past shoulder-length. From her angle, Willow believed most of his hair had been pulled back and secured at his neck. A few strands had escaped confinement, however, and were resting on his wide shoulders. His thick, muscular arms were accentuated by a sleeveless top. Willow's gaze continued lower. The way his jeans hugged his legs made her wonder if he had painted them on. Her mouth watered as she thought about finding out just what he had inside of those jeans.

Almost as an afterthought, she glanced at the second man. This one was blond, a little bit shorter than the brunette and appeared to have a smaller build—though not by much. Although he was handsome, her attention constantly strayed back to the brunette.

The two men neared their table and Willow continued to watch them, her eyes narrowing slightly as she tried to see them more clearly since the lighting around them was dim. With every step that brought the handsome stranger closer, her mouth watered more. She knew this was a man she wouldn't mind getting a taste of, the one she would choose to play her sister's game with.

As he passed by her position at the small table, he almost brushed against her. Willow had to fight the temptation to simply reach out and grab his ass. Ordinarily, she'd never have to restrain the urge to do something that impulsive. Especially not with a perfect stranger.

The men moved past the table too quickly for her. Turning slightly in her chair so she could continue to watch them, she took solace in the delightful view of his firm ass in those wonderfully tight jeans. She didn't try to be discreet as she watched them to see which table they sat at. Her smile widened when they chose one not too far from her friends. The sexy stranger's table was in a wonderfully shadowed corner. It would be perfect for when she swooped in.

Her reluctance to play was forgotten as she focused solely on her target. She even briefly considered thanking her sister for coercing her into the game in the first place.

"I do believe our little Willow's made her choice." Mary drew Willow's attention. "Which one is it? The brunette or the blond?" From her position at the table, Mary was able to watch both men without having to move her chair a single inch.

Looking the two men over once more—only so she didn't appear too anxious or eager—Willow sighed. As far as she was concerned, there was no contest; the gorgeous brunette would win every time. "The brunette," she told the women as casually as she could, doing her best to hide her growing excitement.

"Do you remember the rules?" Mary's glance darted back and forth between Willow and her prey. A knowing smile tilted the corners of her mouth.

Willow nodded.

"We'll go over them anyway," Roxy stated. "Rule one..."

Willow sighed again. She didn't want to waste precious time going over their stupid rules. She wanted to go meet her handsome stranger. "Rule one," she began in a bored voice. "Make sure he isn't attached. This is about fun, not starting trouble or intruding on a relationship."

"Make sure he's not gay either. What?" Mary looked at Willow innocently when Willow glared at her. "These days you never know. There's nothing wrong with being gay, but I think it would be a bit embarrassing if Will tried to kiss him and he told her he was."

"I agree." Roxy nodded. "Don't forget to find out if he's gay."

"Gee, that won't be awkward at all," Willow said sarcastically.

Her sister ignored her. "On to rule two."

"Rule number two, you have to ask permission to join them. If the guy says yes, you have to sit on your target's lap."

"Good. And rule three, the single most important rule?"

"Rule three, never, ever tell a guy about the game. You never tell your prey what is going on and you never apologize," Willow recited, barely resisting the urge to roll her eyes. "This is a game for women because men have been playing games with us for eons." Willow could almost see the other two women sitting in the sisters' living room months before as they came up with this game and the rules. Roxy had just been humiliated by some loser she'd been dating. She'd come home in tears when the guy's fiancée interrupted their dinner. This game supposedly made her feel better as she and Mary decided it was time for them to begin toying with men. Playing their own games with them.

"See, I told you she was paying attention." Mary laughed. "Now, let's get to the good part. I totally think he has on briefs," Mary predicted, stealing another look at Willow's choice.

"Nope." Roxy shook her head. "I've seen his type, definitely boxers. They want to go for comfort and letting it all hang out."

"Commando," Willow responded breathily when she looked over her shoulder at her target once again. She hadn't realized she had spoken aloud until she noticed the look of amusement and mischief the other women were giving her.

Her sister's smile broadened. "You know what that means don't you, sis?"

"Yes, Roxy, I know." Willow glanced at her sister, her patented patient look on her face. The one that silently asked, do you think I'm an idiot? Sometimes it was a blessing to have her sister as one of her very best friends. Others it was a curse. She wasn't sure which category it fell into tonight. After all, if the woman hadn't goaded her into playing, she probably would have called it a night and left before he entered the bar. *But, then again Roxy did just have to agree to add that "ask him if he's gay" part in, didn't she?*

"And just think, you didn't even want to come out tonight." Roxy smirked.

"Well it's time. Take one last sip of your drink. We'll be right here if you need us, sweetie, anxiously waiting for every juicy detail," Mary teased. Her tone grew serious. "If you get uncomfortable at all, just wave and we'll be over there to help in no time."

"And let's not forget the best part of the game. If you kiss, you have got to tell all!"

Willow obeyed her friend and took one final sip of her Alabama Slammer to steel herself for her task. She mumbled thanks as she ignored her sister's final comment. Closing her eyes she got up slowly then—no longer staring at her sister's smirk—turned to approach her intended target.

I cannot believe I let them talk me into this. What was I thinking? I can't do this... I'm going to turn back and tell them I've changed my mind. Who cares if they tease me, it'll be better than making a complete fool out of myself in front of some strange and totally gorgeous guy...

Her body disagreed. Before she could make her legs stop and turn her around, she was standing beside the stranger's table, directly between the blond and the brunette.

"Excuse me..." She forced a smile onto her face as her voice trembled. Leaning closer to the brunette so he could hear her over the music blaring from the speakers on stage, she continued. "I was just wondering if you would mind answering a couple of questions for me?" Willow was grateful for the few small sips of the drink that she had been able to get before she left the table. *Of course, if I had known I'd be playing their crazy game, I'd be on my third drink by now.*

When his clear blue eyes stared up at her, she felt her knees quiver. *God, he looks even more delicious up close.* Willow felt a blush creep up her cheeks when his full lips curved into a devastating smile.

"Not at all," her target replied as the blond sighed audibly and took a sip from his drink.

"Are you married?" He shook his head, an amused smile on his face. A wave of relief washed over her. Now she just had to hope her luck held out. "Do you have a girlfriend?" Again, his answer was no. "Are you gay?" she asked quickly, the words coming out so fast she hoped he hadn't quite heard her question.

Thankfully he didn't ask her to repeat the question. Instead he once again shook his head, though one eyebrow did cock up and his smile dimmed a bit. She took a deep breath in relief.

Time for the next step.

"May I join you?" Willow fought the urge to nervously twist her hair. She was too old for those coy schoolgirl tricks. Clasping her hands behind her back, she attempted to resist the childish temptation. Waiting for his answer, she wished she had taken the time to style her long hair rather than leaving it to hang freely.

"Of course." Her gorgeous prey sounded intrigued and slightly amused.

The guy's friend laughed as she lifted her leg and straddled the guy's lap. Her guy looked even more intrigued. His hands rested on her hips and she was thankful he hadn't pushed her off his lap. She'd seen it happen occasionally to Mary and Roxy and knew she'd be humiliated if it happened to her.

She knew she would get teased for this particular decision when she returned to the table. The rules only stated that you were required to sit on the man's lap; nowhere did they specify *how* you had to sit on the man's lap.

But since this is the only time I will ever play this game, why not follow Roxy's suggestion and have a little fun? I had a hell of a day, and maybe I do feel like playing after all.

"My name is Willow," she said, finally introducing herself.

"It's a pleasure to meet you. I'm Seth." His voice was deep and came out almost like a purr. His hands remained on her hips, caressing her, teasing her ass with their slight touch.

"I was wondering if you would mind answering just one more personal question for me..."

"Come on Seth, there will be enough time to play after we talk," the blond complained. "Just ask your new friend to come back in about twenty minutes."

"Jason, relax. There will still be plenty of time to talk about business in a few minutes. How often do I have the pleasure of having a beautiful lady sit down on my lap?"

Seth spoke to the other man without taking his gaze away from her. He adjusted her body until she was pressed firmly against him, as intimately as possible while they were both still fully dressed. The move sent a shock of desire straight through Willow's body. Moisture pooled between her legs.

"Do you really want me to answer that? Because I believe the answer is last night."

Willow felt another blush creep up from a combination of the other man's remark and the hot look Seth was giving her. He looked as though he wanted to devour her, and she had a feeling she would enjoy every second of it.

"What would you like to know, sweetheart?" Seth was clearly ignoring his friend.

Now that the time had come to ask him her question, she felt more than a little embarrassed. She wanted to explain what was going on. To tell him that it was just a game. But it was against the rules.

Leaning closer to his ear, Willow wanted to hiss with pleasure as her nipples tightened deliciously beneath her shirt when they brushed against his hard chest. She inhaled deeply, enjoying the spicy, sensual smell of him. It reminded her of sex. *No,* she corrected herself. *He doesn't smell like just any sex... He smells like passionate sex, the kind that makes you wonder if you'll ever be able to walk again. And not care if the answer is no...*

Resisting the urge to take his earlobe into her mouth, she softly asked, "Are you wearing boxers or briefs?"

Mimicking her, Seth leaned closer. His body moved against her and made her dizzy with desire. "Sorry, sweetheart, I'm not wearing either." He took her earlobe into his mouth for a quick nibble before slowly releasing it.

Beneath her, Willow felt his cock pressing hard against her as she squirmed from the unexpected kiss. She didn't doubt that he was being honest with her. More moisture gathered between her legs, increasing her anticipation of their kiss.

She was more grateful than he would ever know to discover she had guessed correctly.

If he had told her boxers, she would have been forced to just walk away—according to the rules. Briefs and she could have given him a kiss on the cheek and said thanks. But only because neither of those were her guess. A correct guess meant the guy got a quick kiss on the lips and her phone number. It was one reason she'd been so picky about her target. There was always a chance she would hear from her prey again and she wanted to be certain she wouldn't cringe if he called.

But commando was always rewarded, even if the player had guessed incorrectly. Instead of a quick kiss, she now had an excuse to give him any kiss she wanted. She couldn't wait to taste him, to feel his tongue playing with hers. She had no doubt that he'd return the kiss.

Placing her hands on his chest, Willow leaned back slightly, careful to keep her movements and touch light. Caressing her way up his body until her arms were around his neck, she shifted her position on his lap once again. As the band began the opening chords of a new song—one of their rare slow songs—she leaned in for her kiss.

If she surprised him, it was hard to tell. Seth quickly responded. He opened his mouth and immediately tried to take control of the kiss. He traced his tongue over her lower lip, tempting her to open her mouth more and allow him inside. Before he could become the aggressor, Willow took control. She slid her tongue into his mouth where it played, thrusting and sweeping with the beat of the music around her.

Her entire body could feel the throb of the music as it settled deep inside her while Seth allowed his hands to roam over her body. She felt his hands slide up and down the length of her thighs then withdraw to skim over her hips and around to cup her ass. Combined with the most delicious, knee-melting kiss she'd ever had, she had to struggle to keep her hips still, to prevent herself from dry-humping him in front of the large crowd.

As the kiss continued, Willow felt her body grow hotter, wetter. Almost chocking on a whimper, she craved more of his touch when he moved one hand off her ass and leisurely up her thigh, stopping just before he reached beneath her miniscule skirt. Seth's slightly callused fingers played on her thigh and she began to make small thrusting motions, trying to entice him to continue his exploration. She came close to losing herself in the pleasure of his touch when he obeyed her silent plea, his hand slowly sliding up and down her thigh, coming close but never quite touching her where she needed him to the most.

The slow movement of his hand was a stark contrast to the throbbing beat of the music. The stark contrast of stimulus was the only thing preventing Willow from abandoning herself to the music, to the sensations he created within her and the fire that was now raging through her blood.

Their kiss ended and Willow took a deep breath. She wasn't sure how she was going to manage the return trip to the table where her friends sat. Surely her bones had melted from his kiss, from his touch. After a few minutes, when she finally attempted to stand, Seth gently pulled her back down onto his lap.

"I'll call you tomorrow, Seth." The voice behind her sounded resigned.

Willow's body tensed as the other man reminded they had an audience. She couldn't believe how completely she'd forgotten about his friend as Seth moved his hand beneath her skirt.

"I can see we aren't going to get any work done tonight," the blond continued. He seemed either unaware or uncaring of her embarrassment. "Later."

It took a moment of intense concentration—made harder as Seth caressed her hips where he held her on top of him—before Willow remembered Seth had called the man Jason.

Nodding once, Seth let the other man know he had heard him. But his gaze never once left hers.

Turning her head slightly to try to get a glimpse of their audience, she caught Jason standing and walking away from the table. He'd left them alone.

She tried to get up again, this time a bit more confident that she wouldn't simply fall flat on her face, thanks in large part to the quick return of reality she had just experienced. Once again he easily held her in place. Beneath her, his erection strained to press closer to her.

"Now it's your turn, sweetheart. What are you wearing under your skirt?" Seth placed his hand below her skirt, allowing it to travel up her thigh and stopping just shy of touching her. His hands played delicious havoc on her senses as he began drawing circles on her flesh with one finger, so very close to where Willow knew she was dripping for him.

Practically moaning, it was a struggle not to begin writhing on his lap as her senses were overloaded with pleasure.

"Tell me, what will I find if I touch you?" His breath tickled her ear.

Nothing. I don't like wearing underwear and tonight I'm really, really glad they annoy me. She closed her eyes, amazed the man wasn't sitting in a puddle of her juices. When was the last time any man made her this hot, this horny?

"May I find out?"

This was it, the time for her to say no or call her friends over if she wanted to simply walk away from him. Looking into Seth's eyes, she couldn't stop herself from finding out what his touch would feel like there, on her bare pussy. It had been too long—it felt like an eternity—since she was last touched by a handsome man. Nodding almost eagerly, she let him—and the two women she knew to be watching them avidly—see that she gave her consent.

Willow closed her eyes and tried to forget about her friends. The other women were the last thing she needed to be thinking about at that moment. *They may not see exactly what he's doing, but with their dirty minds, they should be able to guess rather accurately...* She was amazed when there was no accompanying embarrassment with the thought. Opening her eyes she waited for his touch.

Not for the first time since she'd picked him, Willow was thankful he had chosen a semi-dark corner to sit in. Without taking his eyes off hers, Seth moved his hand the short distance to where she was hot, wet, and thanks to her straddling his lap, open for him.

His fingers had barely skimmed her slit, stroking only the outer edges of her lips when she grew wetter. *Much more of this and he really will be sitting in a puddle.*

He moved his finger back and forth, caressing the outer folds of her sex as her hips flexed, encouraging him to touch more of her, to slide his finger deeper. When he finally parted her folds, barely grazing her clit, Willow's eyes closed blissfully. Arching closer to him, she reveled in the erotic sensations he seemed to awaken in her body, gasping, praying for more.

Taking advantage of her gasp, Seth swooped down on her. His tongue plunged deep into her mouth, thrusting aggressively as he mimicked the motion of his fingers stroking and lightly pinching her clit.

Moaning deep in her throat from the pleasure of his touch, she shifted her hips against him, tilting her body slightly to allow him better access to her pussy. His attention transferring from her mouth back to her ear, Seth nibbled on her lobe as his hand continued bringing her pleasure.

Finally answering her silent plea, he easily slid one of his fingers inside of her, forcing her to bite down on her lip or moan aloud. When he added another, her head fell backward from the pleasure as her hands gripped his shoulders. Seth's fingers thrust in and out of her, matching the rhythm of the song the band was now playing. Eagerly, Willow arched her hips to meet him, all thoughts of discretion fleeing.

He pressed his thumb against her, continuing to tease her clit. His movements followed the increasing tempo of the song, causing her to bite her lip harder as she lost her grip on reality.

Thankfully, as the first telltale signs of her impending orgasm began, Seth claimed her mouth. His tongue stole the moans that threatened to escape as her body tensed, pulling him deeper inside of her.

Willow was sucking on his tongue as greedily as her pussy gripped his fingers, an orgasm tearing through her body.

Burying her head in his shoulder, she sent up a silent prayer of thanks that there had been a band playing at the bar, distracting the other patrons from whatever happened in their corner of the room.

CRED

Seth was as hard as a rock beneath her. Lifting her head up so he could look into her sated eyes, he placed another brief kiss on Willow's lips. Despite the amazing orgasm he had just brought her to, she arched into his body, as though she wanted to find out how he would feel deep inside her.

He was more than willing to show her. He was anxious to find out how her tight, wet pussy would feel milking his cock the way it tried to milk his fingers.

Looking around, he thought he could always use the back office for a quickie... But he didn't want to do that. He wanted time to savor her. *Would she be willing to return to my home where I could take my time ravishing her body?*

He refused to look inside her mind, didn't want to invade her thoughts to discover what he wished to know. With her it felt somehow wrong.

Paying attention to her expression, he watched her closely as she rested her head on his shoulder, her face flushed with passion. She had blushed so prettily as she questioned him, then again when she realized Jason was still at the table while she kissed him. It had given her an air of innocence. One that quickly melted away when she'd kissed him the first time.

Her mouth tasted sweet, full of passion and honesty. If her blood tasted the same, he knew he would not wish to part ways with her after only one encounter...

No, Seth's mind was made up. He wouldn't insult her by taking her into the dust-covered room labeled his office, or even to a hotel. Thinking hard, he knew most women wouldn't be comfortable telling someone they just met where they lived. On an impulse, he decided to take her to his apartment. At least then he could be sure they would have no interruptions. Especially when he drank from her. There, he would have the luxury of taking his time, of making sure her body was fully sated as he tasted every inch of her.

Without saying a word, Seth held on to her hips and stood, smiling when she pouted at the loss of his body pressed so intimately against hers. When her legs appeared to once again accept her weight, he took her hand. Leading her through the crowd, he maneuvered them toward the exit. She followed willingly. He hoped that, like him, she couldn't wait to feel him touching her so much more. Outside of the bar, it was a short walk to where he'd parked his motorcycle. Not for the first time, he praised the convenience of the machine, knowing it would help get him to his home as quickly as possible.

Being a gentleman, Seth helped her to climb on the machine before he placed the spare helmet on her head. When he sat in front of her, Willow wrapped her arms around his waist. In no time the engine was purring beneath them, and they were on their way.

Another thing he loved about his motorcycle was the way a person could feel the motor purring through their body. He knew the vibrations from the engine would bring her clit humming back to life almost instantly.

Willow pressed herself tight against him. She slid her cheek back and forth against his shirt as she gently stroked his stomach. More than once Seth had to remind himself to pay attention as he drove.

He wanted her to do more, feel her body against his bare flesh, but knew it would be safer to wait until they were no longer on a moving vehicle. They would both be denied too much if he had an accident.

In no more than five minutes he'd parked the bike in an underground parking deck, dismounted and ushered her over to a waiting elevator. Climbing inside, he inserted then twisted his key into the special section of the elevator. After he pushed the button that would take them to his apartment, he returned his attention to her.

Pulling Willow close, he once again began his teasing caresses on her skin as the doors closed. There was no chance of them getting caught since the elevator wouldn't stop until it reached his floor, but Seth wondered if the idea of being discovered would make his tempting new friend wetter.

Sliding his hands under her shirt, he effortlessly unhooked her bra. Pulling the silk and lace item apart, he slipped each strap off her shoulder and, with Willow's help, down her arms. Once the barrier was removed, and her bra tucked safely inside the pocket of his jeans, he reached back under her shirt and cupped her breasts. He moved his thumbs back and forth, teasing her nipples until they were tight buds and Willow was leaning into his hands, eager for more.

Chapter Two

Willow watched in shock as Seth knelt on the elevator floor in front of her. Lifting her shirt, he kissed one erect nipple before shifting to the other, circling it with his tongue. Sucking the already tight bud into his mouth, he looked up into her face.

She knew desire was written all over her expression. How could it not be with the things he had done—was doing to her body?

A very low moan escaped her throat as he teased first one breast then the other. Her breasts ached with desire. She wasn't sure how much longer she could wait to feel him inside of her. Back and forth he altered his focus, making certain each breast received equally lavish attention.

After what felt like an eternity, the elevator finally stopped, bringing Willow back to reality once again. How was he able to make her lose herself so completely? Never before had she become so wrapped up in what was happening to her that she'd forgotten completely about her surroundings. Yet Seth had managed to make her forget everything but him twice that evening. What if there had been another stop, and another person—or couple—had joined them inside the small car?

Seth stood quickly and, without warning, picked her up. The feel of his arms so strong around her forced her to forget her previous embarrassment. He carried her through the apartment, not pausing to show her anything, but she didn't mind. She was too entranced with this man who wove such a spell on her that she didn't bother to look around and see what his home was like.

In what felt like a few short seconds, she was standing on her own again. Glancing around, she saw she was inside of his bedroom, by a bed that—when she turned to look at it—she noticed was decadently huge.

Watching him avidly, Willow felt her mouth water as Seth pulled off his shirt, revealing a well-muscled chest with just the right amount of hair covering it. She wouldn't feel as though she were in bed with a bear, but there was plenty for her to twist her fingers in as she enjoyed nibbling on his nipples. Sitting on the bed, Seth removed his shoes next. Willow looked back up at his face, desire still coursing through her. She was surprised to find his steady gaze on her, as though he were gauging her reaction to him.

Reason once again tried to intrude on her pleasure. *How did things get this far this fast? Is this really what I want?* Questions assailed her as she pondered the wisdom of allowing things to move so quickly. She wasn't used to jumping into one-night stands.

After the unbelievable orgasm he'd given her in the bar, surrounded by people, Willow was sure he was a talented lover. No one had ever made her feel that way while in a crowded room before. Never before had she been even remotely tempted to leave a bar with a man she had just met.

Her gaze feasted on what she could see of his bare body as he stood, and the sensible side of her wondered if she should put a stop to things before his mouth made her forget everything but him once more.

Her gaze followed the trail of soft brown hair leading down to the waistband of his jeans and she licked her lips. Seth paused, grasping the button, ready to open his pants or possibly to stop if she were to give the slightest protest.

Sensing his hesitation made her decision easier. Tonight she would forget she was the mature sister. Tonight she would be immature and selfish, taking what she wanted. And she wanted Seth. She gave herself permission to have fun and not to question every minor action, to do things that she would typically be entirely too embarrassed to try. Walking over to him, she eased his hands away from their position then unbuttoned his jeans herself as she rose to her tiptoes to place a tender kiss on his lips.

Pulling slightly away from him, she easily played the part of temptress when he tried to coax her into a deeper kiss. Tugging his jeans low, she felt them fall off of his hips. With a single step back, Willow admired the body now bared completely to her.

Her eyes widened as she stared at him. Having him beneath her, erect but still fully dressed, had not prepared her for just how blessed he was down there. He was huge! His cock was long, thick and hard, and it looked as if it were ready to attack.

His body is truly amazing. To let a body like this *go to waste is shameful.*

Stepping closer, she allowed her fingers to skim down his hard body. She was unable to feel so much as an ounce of spare fat on him. His muscles tensed beneath her light touch. Finally taking his erection into her hand, she stroked the velvety flesh while he looked down at her.

She felt powerful and seductive. A smile tilted Willow's lips. Lowering herself to her knees on the hardwood floor, she licked the single fat drop of moisture from the silky tip.

Seth's groan of pleasure encouraged her to continue. Guiding his cock to her lips, she traced the head with her tongue before sucking him into her mouth. She stroked him that way for a few moments, her tongue moving against the soft underside as he withdrew from her. Willow was careful to savor any moisture that escaped him. She whimpered when his hands stopped her ministrations.

"Ah, sweetheart, if you keep that up we'll both be disappointed," he told her. His voice was husky with desire as he pulled himself from her mouth while she pouted.

Pulling her up his body, Seth kissed Willow's bottom lip, taking it into his mouth, ruining her pout. When the kiss ended, her shirt was off and thrown somewhere—she believed it was across the room. Her shoes and miniskirt soon followed. She wasn't sure exactly how he managed to strip her so quickly, unable to process much of anything other than the assault on her senses. She wondered if the pleasure portion of her brain was being overloaded.

Seth picked her up once again, and crossed the remaining slight distance to his sinful bed. Seconds after he lowered her to the mattress, he joined her, his body pressing hers deeper into the soft bedding. He resumed his earlier teasing of her breasts, palming them as he kissed her deeply. Her hips arched against him and this time he was the one with a wicked grin. His mouth set a trail of fire coursing down her body everywhere it touched. She raised her hips, inviting him closer when he nipped her flesh. When she arched up, he winked at her before continuing his delicious torture. Willow was ready to end all games, to pin him to the bed, as her pussy ached to feel him buried deep inside of her.

Unmindful of how badly she wanted him at the moment, Seth seemed content to take his time. He slid his hand slowly up her leg, caressing her flesh before teasing and stroking her sex. Biting down on her lip, she closed her eyes and arched her hips as he slid his finger deep inside of her, and thrust gently.

"Oh, sweetheart, you're so wet. I want to taste you," he murmured, his head close to her pussy. The second the words left his mouth, his finger was replaced by his tongue.

He parted her folds, and allowed his thumb to circle her straining clit. Raising his mouth slightly, he pressed two fingers deep within her as he suckled the small bud into his mouth.

"You taste like honey." His breath wreaked havoc on her as it met her damp flesh.

She wasn't sure what exactly turned her on more; his words, his mouth or his fingers. What was it about him that made her lose control so completely? Never before had talking dirty made her this wet, but then everything Seth did to her—everything he said—made her want him more.

"Oh God." The moan escaped her when she felt herself straining, her muscles tensing as she felt another orgasm approaching.

"What would you like, sweetheart?" Seth sucked on her swollen bud once before continuing. "What do you want?"

"I want to feel you," she pleaded. "All of you inside of me. Please."

"But I am inside you," he teased. He thrust his fingers into her once again as though to remind her.

"Your cock," she gasped. "I want your cock inside me." Somehow she was getting even hotter by admitting what she wanted to him.

"Inside you where?" He tortured her with another quick stroke of his tongue gliding over her clit. Raising his head slightly, he continued talking. "In your mouth?" He swirled his tongue around her clit. "Your sweet little ass?" He repeated the gesture, his fingers leaving her to glide over her skin and grasp one ass cheek in his hand before they lingered on—but never entered—the pucker. "Mmmm, or your tight pussy?" Once again he lowered his mouth to suckle her clit and thrust his fingers deep inside her.

"Oh, God," she moaned loudly as his actions continued to drive her crazy. "In my...in my pussy," she gasped. "Please, God, in my pussy, now." She pleaded with him, tangling her fingers in his hair and lifting her hips against his mouth.

He ignored her request, thrusting his fingers inside her until she was so close to orgasm she couldn't think.

Just as her muscles began to tense around him, he stopped and quickly crawled up her body. At the loss of his touch Willow's eyes opened and she saw him rolling a condom down his cock. Positioning himself at her dripping entrance, his enormous cock was buried deep inside of her with a single thrust. Biting down on her already sensitive lip, Willow almost drew blood when his entrance triggered her orgasm.

Seth somehow remained still, unmoving inside her until she felt the waves of pleasure beginning to ease.

The sensation of being filled by him was incredible, and he was being so gentle. She was still dripping from her desire for him, her body still needy for him. Soon she couldn't take it anymore. She shifted beneath him to feel him move and dug her nails into his back.

Following her cue, he thrust into her, keeping his pace slow, teasing; driving her crazy yet again with desire. Willow sucked her lip into her mouth, intending to bite down on it, but Seth surprised her. He stopped the abuse by kissing her deeply, his teeth grazing against her lip slightly. He slid his tongue over her lip before plunging it into her mouth.

Wrapping her legs around his hips she met him thrust for thrust. Her nails scored his back with every pass. Finally, mercifully, Seth increased the speed of his thrusts. Moving her hands lower, she grasped his firm ass, pulling him harder against her, unable to get enough.

Thankfully her movements only seemed to encourage him. His pace increased again, his thrusts becoming ever more forceful. Panting, she pressed her mouth to his shoulder as yet another orgasm came over her body.

Her entire body trembled, her muscles twitching beneath her flesh and after just a few more strokes, he growled then stilled within her.

Floating back down to her body, Willow noticed that he took care to keep most of his weight on his arms rather than crushing her. Truthfully, she wouldn't have minded if he rested fully on her. Her legs felt as though they were made of jelly, but she locked her ankles, keeping them wrapped around his waist, unwilling to give up the feeling of his cock inside her just yet.

Seth seemed to understand her desire because he wrapped his arms around her and rolled, positioning them so she was sitting on top of him as he remained buried deep inside her.

Willow watched contently as Seth reached up and cupped her breasts, his thumbs stroking her nipples. Unconsciously she bit down on her lower lip again. Releasing one breast, he lifted his hand, allowing his finger to trace the abused lip.

"Don't fight what you feel," he told her as his thumb caressed her lip. "Why do you bite your lip?"

She was embarrassed by his question, the answer an awkward one. "It's just something I started doing." His left eyebrow rose, but Seth never stopped fondling her breast leisurely.

"Tell me?" he asked gently.

With a sigh, she relented. "One of my exes complained that I was too...vocal. It was...embarrassing. So, I've just bitten my lip to keep my moans inside ever since."

"The man was a fool. There is no sweeter sound than the moan of desire from a woman's lips." He removed his thumb from her lip and moved it between them, rubbing her sensitive clit. Unable stop herself, Willow began to bite her lip again.

Seth removed his other hand from her breast, sliding his thumb across her mouth, stopping her from abusing the lip further.

"Let me hear you. I want to hear how much I please you."

She was stunned. Not once since that asshole complained, had any man asked to hear her.

"Will you let me hear you?" Seth moved his hand back to her breast.

Struggling, she barely resisted the urge to bite her lip. *I've been holding my moans inside for so long, I'm not even sure if I can give in to his request.*

He increased the pressure and speed of his fingers across her sensitive clit and she felt a moan beginning deep inside her.

Almost as if he knew she needed help, Seth pulled her down into a kiss. As he sucked on her abused lower lip, she moaned. He was gentle with her, his tongue easing any pain she felt. She wanted to moan more for him. Moving his lips down past her neck to her breast, he gently bit her pebbled nipple and she let another moan escape her mouth. It felt good to be free to express her desire, her pleasure.

"Do you feel what your moans do to me?" Taking one of her hands, he placed it between their bodies at the base of his cock. As her fingers pressed against him, she could feel him growing hard beneath her touch. It was a heady sensation. She'd never felt a man harden with her hand while he was still buried deep inside of her. His hand remained over hers. Guiding it higher, he arranged her fingers so they brushed against her clit. He encouraged her to touch herself, to tease her body.

Willow pulled her hand back, embarrassed. Though she had pleasured herself in the past when a lover had left her less than satisfied, never before had anyone ever watched her do it.

"Don't fight it. Let me watch you give yourself pleasure. Show me what you like," he coaxed.

Willow bit her lip again, this time from nervousness. She moved her fingers against her sex, moaning as she caressed herself the way she liked. The sensation of her fingers tugging her clit was made more erotic and intense as Seth grew harder inside of her while he watched her movements. His eyes held no condemnation, only intense desire. Quickening her pace, she shifted her hips, moving against him and creating a delicious friction.

His hand covered hers once again as he forced her to slow her movements. "Not yet, sweetheart, not yet. Allow me to enjoy watching you a little longer. I want you to go slowly, teasing yourself...teasing me. Make both of our bodies tremble."

Nodding, Willow forced herself to decrease her speed. She tried to concentrate on keeping her pace slow instead of on the pleasure building inside of her. She moaned, slightly louder than before as another orgasm built, but did her best to deny the climax. Willow shut her eyes. Her head fell back as she continued the leisurely pace.

Her moans increased as he lifted slightly from beneath her and suckled on her breast. He traced his tongue in a pattern over one sensitive nipple as he pinched the other between his fingers. Willow struggled to remain still. Her entire body seemed to scream for her to move against the hard cock inside of her.

"Oh, God," she moaned.

"A bit longer, sweetheart," he groaned around her nipple.

"Seth, I need you."

"Just a little longer."

Opening her eyes, Willow looked at him. More than anything she wanted to stop, to move her hand and begin to ride him, finally allowing herself to orgasm as she pressed his head closer to her body. But she obeyed him. She continued to stroke herself, but could no longer keep her hips still. Willow started thrusting against him with each stroke she gave to herself. She tilted her head to the side, watching him feast on her. Her moans came louder and faster, pleading for release.

He lay back down on the bed. His hands gripped her ass and allowed him to direct her movements.

"That's it, let yourself go." He encouraged her as he increased the pressure on her hips, speeding her motions.

Willow pulled her hand away from her body, intending to pull him back to her, but he quickly stopped her.

"Not yet. You aren't done yet."

When she didn't put her hand back immediately, Seth stopped thrusting and lifted her off his hips, withdrawing himself. When she stared at him confused, he smiled. Her attempts to lower herself back onto him were met with resistance.

"Not until you begin to please yourself again," he whispered.

Wasting no time, she put her fingers back on her dripping pussy. Feeling a bit mischievous herself, Willow stuck a finger in her pussy, wiping the juices on her swollen clit as she slowly slid her fingers across. Seth pulled her back down onto his cock, once again filling her completely.

Watching his face closely, she smiled. Seth seemed excited by what she had just done. Taking a chance, she switched hands and lifted the finger with her cream on it to his mouth. Slipping her finger past his lips, Willow increased her speed as he sucked on her finger hungrily.

"Oh, yes," she moaned. "Harder."

Seth pulled her hard against him but it wasn't enough.

"Harder," she moaned again.

With a growl, Seth pulled her hand away and, rolling them over, he shifted her legs to his shoulders. Holding most of his weight on his arms, he began to pound inside of her.

"Oh, God, yes," she cried out. Willow curled her fingers, her nails digging into his arms but neither paid any attention. They were both too lost in the sensations to stop. He was thrusting inside her hard and fast, and she loved it, raising her hips to meet him with as much force as she was able to manage. The harder he thrust, the louder her moans became and the more intense her pleasure. This time as an orgasm ripped through her body she swore she saw stars coming to life. Within seconds

Seth collapsed on top of her, his breathing ragged and muscles trembling beneath her touch.

CR8O

No woman has made me lose control like this in a very long time! He was exhausted.

Lying on top of her, he was completely spent, unable to even hold his weight off her because every muscle was shaking as he fought desperately to regain control of his body.

He had lost count long ago of how many years had passed since any woman had affected his body as Willow had that night. He wasn't even sure *if* any other woman *had* made him lose control as fully as he just had with her. Seth's teeth lengthened, wanting to taste her more fully. But he forced himself to wait. There would be time enough to satisfy that particular craving after he made sure she was well satisfied. He had never left a lady unfulfilled, and wouldn't start now. Besides, if the small sample of blood he had tasted during one of their kisses could cause such havoc on his senses, how much more would truly drinking from her affect him?

Finally getting his hunger under control, he rolled off her, not missing her low whimper when he moved. Pulling slightly away, he removed the well-used condom and dropped it into a trashcan he kept beside his bed. When that chore was completed, he pulled her close, fitting her body tight against his. Propping his head on one arm, he draped the other across her waist and stroked her stomach.

This woman was a true delight. Never would he have dared hope for such a wildcat in bed. Even now, knowing his body would need a little time to recuperate before he could once again bury himself within her, he felt his lust for her stirring.

She turned and looked back at him, a look of wonder on her face.

"What's going through your mind, sweetheart?" And he really did want to know. That was another thing that surprised him—how much he did not want to simply pry into her mind.

"I was just wondering if I should get dressed," Willow answered honestly.

Her answer confused him. Usually he was the one who was ready for the woman to leave. Never before had a woman wished to jump straight out of his bed like that. "Why?"

"So you can take me home."

Looking down at her, he resisted the urge to sigh. He even managed to control the more difficult to resist temptation of probing her mind and seeing what was going on inside of her. He wasn't ready for her to leave yet, but the decision to stay had to be hers. If she wished for him to take her home that night he would oblige her. Free will was a big deal with his people.

"Do you *want* me to take you home now?" He kept his tone gentle, as though he weren't screaming inside for her to stay. Every part of him protested that he had not had nearly enough of her yet.

She lay there a moment, clearly thinking about his question and what answer she should give. After what felt like an eternity to him, she shook her head. "I'd like to stay here if you don't mind."

"Then it's settled." Leaning down, he claimed her mouth in a gentle kiss. "Get some rest, sweetheart. This is going to be a night filled with pleasure."

"You, sir, are going to spoil me." Willow stretched in front of him, reminding him of a feline, well satisfied with life.

An odd sensation settled in his stomach when Willow shifted, laying her head on his arm after he lowered it. Within moments, her regular breathing told him she was fast asleep.

He smiled as she snuggled closer to him, even in her sleep. The simple action let him know better than words could that she hadn't had enough of him yet either.

A few hours later Seth woke her by stroking her body. He could tell by the amazed look on her face she wasn't used to such an energetic lover.

Without meaning to, he heard her thoughts. *He is definitely different from my previous lovers.* She was purring in her thoughts.

He hadn't intentionally eavesdropped on her thoughts, but that didn't stop the wave of pride that washed over him at the praise and awe in them.

Wasting no time, he determined to live up to her admiration, and soon had her moaning and pleading for him to fill her again.

As he continued to caress her body, Seth felt satisfaction in the knowledge that he stirred her lust so completely. Thrusting into her, he felt like a young man once again, as though he couldn't get enough of her. Briefly he wondered if their coupling would be equally passionate many years into the future.

Before he could question where the unexpected thought came from, he felt Willow clenching around him, pushing his controls to the limit until he was ready to explode inside of her.

Rolling onto his side he gathered Willow into his arms, thankful he had decided to go to the bar that night.

Chapter Three

Willow stretched her body, lazily enjoying the wonderfully stiff and sore feeling. She prayed the previous night had been real and not just some wet dream.

A hand slid up her leg as she stretched, renewing her confidence that what she'd felt had indeed been real.

Cracking one eye open, she saw the hottie from the bar. Smiling, she opened both eyes fully. The room was somewhat dark from the curtains, but she could see him clearly, thanks to a nearby lamp he must have cut on.

"Good morning," she said, her voice sounding like a purr even to her own ears.

Seth looked enticing in his snug black jeans and white shirt. His hair was still damp, and combed back from his face, letting her know he had showered while she slept.

"Good morning. Did you sleep well?"

Nodding, Willow felt blood rush to her face as she remembered the things she had done the previous night. She began to chew on her lip.

"Ah, sweetheart, you do abuse that lip." He leaned down and slid his thumb over her bottom lip before kissing her, sucking her lip into his mouth and soothing it by gliding his tongue across it.

"Mmmmm," she moaned as she rose to meet him, kissing him back hungrily. His hand was wandering higher, up her thigh and hip to her waist. His fingers blazed a trail of molten desire everywhere they touched her bare flesh. They continued their trek to where the sheet was pulled high on her body, covering her breasts. She would have thought after the many orgasms she experienced the previous night, sex would be the last thing on her mind. She would have been wrong.

Pulling the sheet away from her, he let it fall to her waist. She watched his face while he stared at her. He appeared as though he couldn't get enough of her, as if he were starving for another taste of her.

Smiling seductively, Seth spoke, his voice husky, "You look good enough to eat this morning."

Willow felt her face grow warm with the memory of his mouth between her legs. "I should probably get up," she murmured, but made no effort to shift any farther than to a sitting position.

"That's up to you. You may stay in my bed for as long as you like." Seth smiled at how easily she blushed. This blushing beauty acted different from the brazen lover of the night before, but was just as tempting. True, he had tasted the alcohol on her breath during their first kiss, but he had known she was not drunk. She'd been aware she was coming back to his place when they left the bar or he would never have taken advantage of her.

"Seth? Seth, are you in here?"

Willow moved with a speed that surprised him as she covered herself, blocking her beautiful body from his gaze when footsteps approached his bedroom.

He only barely suppressed a groan. Leave it to Jason to pick just the wrong time to stop by.

"Seth? Oh, there you are." Jason paused, then sounded embarrassed. "I'm sorry. I didn't mean to interrupt anything." Seth heard his friend quickly back out of the room and close the door.

"I should probably let you go," Willow said, sitting a little straighter in the bed.

Unable to stop himself, Seth tuned in to her thoughts.

Not only should I let him go get to whatever business I interrupted last night, but Seth is probably only being polite, telling me I can stay as long as I want.

"I do not say things I do not mean, sweetheart," he told Willow, automatically trying to reassure her. He was still unwilling to have her leave just yet. "Please believe if I wanted you to leave, you would not still be in my bed."

Her surprise at his knowledge of her thoughts showed in her expression. As did her next question. She wanted to know how he knew what she was thinking.

"Your thoughts were written all over your face. And believe me, I would be more than happy to tell Jason that he will have to come back later so I can rejoin you in bed." Leaning his head closer to her, Seth traced the curve of her neck with his tongue before his mouth met her flesh, kissing the spot his tongue had lingered on.

He couldn't resist any longer. The small taste he'd had the night before only seemed to whet his appetite for her.

Carefully, so she couldn't see him, Seth allowed his teeth to lengthen and graze gently against her flesh. When he bit her, she moaned deep in her throat. She twisted her fingers in his hair and held his head close while he suckled her neck. As he began to drink deeply, her head fell back, giving him more access to her. She didn't seem to care if she walked away with a mark, or how dark it would be. Seth kneaded her breast, the feel of her silky skin against his palm increasing his enjoyment in the delicious taste of her blood.

Taking a quick look inside her mind, Seth remained only long enough to assure himself that her thoughts were filled with nothing but pleasure. His fingers found her nipple and grasped it between them. A deep moan left her, tempting him to tell Jason to fuck off so he could enjoy her sweet body once again.

Swirling his tongue against her skin as he gave one last suck, Seth closed the wound and cleaned away any lingering traces of blood. He held his head against her shoulder for a moment, feeling as though he'd just gotten drunk off of her.

"You are more temptation than one man should have," he confessed huskily. He lowered his mouth to press a light kiss on the rosy nipple he'd teased as he drank from her.

"Why don't you go take care of whatever business I've been keeping you from? As soon as I can make my legs work again, I'll get up and take a shower."

"I won't be away for long," he promised. Taking one final, lingering look at her body, he pulled the sheet back up around her, covering her from his gaze. Lifting her hand to his lips, he sucked a finger into his mouth, then placed a lasting kiss on the back of her knuckles. "We'll finish this soon."

Outside of his room, Seth hid in the darkness, watching her through a small crack he'd left when he didn't shut the door fully. Another surge of pride and satisfaction filled him when Willow buried her head in his pillow and took a deep breath, seconds before she fell asleep.

"Jason, to what do I owe this pleasure?" he asked sarcastically as he emerged from the hallway.

"I told you last night I would be by today to finish discussing business with you. I'm not surprised you forgot. You seemed a bit...distracted." Jason sat on the couch and began to open his folders.

"Then let's hurry up and get it over with. I have a very pleasant lady to get back to."

"Of course." Jason pulled out the first paper. "A gentleman has made an offer for The Grunge. It's very generous...more than the place will earn you in ten years."

"I do not wish to sell it."

"May I ask why?"

"No. I simply will not sell it and that is final." Much like his beloved antiques, the small bar held a special place in Seth's heart. Because of its emotional, rather than monetary, value. It had taken him a long time, but over the decades he'd cultivated that place into a safe haven. The patrons there knew they could truly be themselves. And without that bar, several of the small local bands would never have a live audience to practice in front of. He wouldn't see it be turned into another parking garage or suave coffee shop.

"Are you sure you won't reconsider selling the bar?" Jason tried one final time.

Holding back his irritation, Seth knew his friend was only trying to do his job to the best of his ability, but nothing would change his mind. "I'll never change my mind about selling that particular bar. Tell him if he would like to negotiate for any other business I'd be happy to consider his offer. But not that one," Seth stated firmly, leaving no doubt in the other man's mind his decision was final.

For fifteen minutes he listened, completely bored, as Jason brought him up-to-date on any important happenings in his other businesses. His mind continued to return to the beautiful woman lying naked in his bed.

"I believe that about covers all of the business. Would you like me to drop your guest off somewhere?" Jason gathered the papers into a neat stack before he returned them to his folder.

"No," Seth replied, practically growling. "She will stay here for the moment. When she desires to leave, I will take her home."

"Are you sure that's a wise choice?"

Seth's eyes narrowed. He didn't want to think about Jason being left alone with Willow. She was so tempting, so hard to resist. And he'd hate to ruin their friendship by ripping Jason's head from his body.

"We've been friends forever, hell I've known you my whole life. I don't want you to do anything reckless." Now that business was finished, Jason had slipped back into their more usual light and friendly banter.

"I know what I'm doing. I'll be all right." Seth had to force himself to relax and forget about the vicious thoughts from a few seconds earlier.

"Just be careful until dark."

"Yes, Mother," Seth told his friend in a bored voice.

"I guess I'll let you go so that you can get back to whatever it was you were doing with your guest." When Seth opened his mouth, as if to say something, Jason quickly added, "And believe me, I really don't want to know anything about it." He headed for the elevator doors, shaking his head as he entered and pushed a button. "Because that would just be disturbing and gross, like walking in on your parents having sex." Jason shuddered.

Seth couldn't help but laugh at his friend. He was a nearly eight-hundred-year-old vampire, and Jason wasn't thirty yet. But the substantial difference in their ages didn't stop Jason from acting like a mother hen at times. Other times he acted as though he were Seth's own child. Seth couldn't decide which attitude frustrated him more. Or which he found more amusing.

As Seth watched the elevator doors close, he waved. He would be forever grateful for the young man and his family. Every member of Jason's family knew the truth about him. Some of the very few humans to know about his race, they'd helped throw off any suspicions about him many times, often acting as though he were a son no one knew about—or some distant cousin—and helping him blend in. Hell, with help from them, he had been able to convince people he was his own child more times than he cared to admit.

Seth shook his head. He'd had a lonely existence for too long. If not for Jason and his family, he would have gone insane centuries ago. But of all the humans who had helped him over the years, Seth knew he would miss Jason the most when his time on this earth was over. He was tempted to change him, but refused to be selfish. When—or if—Jason ever asked, Seth would gladly grant the man's request. But it had to be Jason's decision. Seth wouldn't coerce him or guilt him into changing merely so he would have company throughout the ages.

Walking over to the control panel he had discreetly hidden in a secret section of the wall, Seth pressed a series of buttons, locking the elevator. Until he unlocked it, the entire floor was blocked. Not even the few people with a key would be able to access his home. Continuing to lock up, he walked over to the mandatory door leading into the stairwell and barred that as well. This was his most vulnerable time—when the sun rose high across the sky.

Smiling, he returned to the hallway leading to his bedroom. All thoughts of loneliness and melancholy left him as his guest's scent drifted up to meet him. Willow's small form was stretched out, spread from one corner to the other at both her head and feet. It was a sight he was sure would make any man's mouth water, and he was no exception.

Moving to the foot of the bed, he gave one tug and the sheet covering her body fell away. His gaze traveled her body, devouring every curve as both his lust and his hunger began to stir yet again. He could practically hear her moans in his ear as her nipples hardened from the slight chill in his room. Sitting on the bed, he stripped off his clothes before leaning over and placing a kiss on her thigh. Unable to stop there, he shifted his position. Lowering himself, he began at her ankle and proceeded to kiss his way up her leg.

Willow sighed with pleasure in her sleep as Seth continued to tease a path higher, until he reached the soft flesh connecting leg to torso. Leaning down, he placed a lingering kiss on the flesh, allowing his tongue to glide over her skin. When he grazed her with his teeth she spread her legs apart, bending the knee and pulling it higher, to give him better access to her.

Seth transferred his attention to the patch of golden curls between her legs. As he scattered kisses above the curls, she let out a sound similar to disappointment.

"What do you want from me, sweetheart?" He was careful to keep his voice low and seductive. He made sure not to put any influence in it; he wanted to know just what she wanted from him as she hovered between sleep and wakefulness.

Willow repositioned her leg again. Dipping his head back down to the smooth juncture, she once again sighed with pleasure. She even reached down, one hand coming to rest lightly on the back of his head. Seth teased her flesh, tracing ancient symbols onto her body. When his teeth grazed against her skin again, she pressed herself up, closer to his mouth.

Intrigued, he took the opportunity to nibble on her, pleased when he heard a moan come out of her mouth. Moving his mouth over her flesh, he paused. Beneath his lips, and tongue as he pressed it against her body, he could feel the blood surging through the vein, teasing him.

She tasted so intoxicating earlier... Seth knew he shouldn't drink from her again, especially not this soon, but had a hard time controlling himself.

Nibbling on the area again, this time biting a little harder, he was rewarded with another moan as her body pressed up against him. Willow twisted her hand into his hair. He gave in to the temptation, to the unspoken, unconscious request she was making.

Seth lost control of himself as her other hand joined with the first, tangling in his hair and holding him tightly against her. His teeth lengthened, sinking easily into the vein that had teased him seconds earlier. He fought to keep his mouth gentle, but drank greedily from her, unable to get enough of her taste.

As he drank, Willow stirred on the bed, her hips lifting restlessly. He could tell the minute she woke, but continued to gently drink from her.

"Oh my." She moaned, beginning to buck her hips underneath him, despite the fact that he had yet to touch her dripping slit with even the barest of caresses.

"What are you doing to me?" Willow asked breathlessly. She was lifting her hips as though he were thrusting into her. She increased the pace of her movements as her fingers formed claws, digging into his scalp with her pleasure. Just as he was about to withdraw his teeth from her body, Willow screamed out, trembling in the aftermath of an orgasm.

With a smooth flick of his tongue, he easily closed the small holes in her skin, but nothing would hide the deep purple mark made by his sucking. It was the only telling sign that he'd drank from her body.

Climbing up on the bed beside her, he lay down, pulling her close to him, her back pressing into his chest. His hands roamed on her body, teasing her nipples and caressing her breasts. He nibbled on her shoulder as he moved his hand, seeking her wet pussy. He tugged her clit, causing her to moan and lean back, pressing tighter against him.

Dipping his fingers into her, he moaned at how wet she was as she surrounded his digits. Lifting her leg, she bent it at the knee, giving him better access to her body.

Seth removed his fingers from her pussy and positioned his hard cock at her dripping entrance. With one hard thrust he was buried completely inside her. His eyes closed and rolled up slightly at just how wonderful she felt wrapped around him. How perfectly they fit together.

"Gods, sweetheart, you're so wet, so tight..." He nibbled on her shoulder. It was a struggle to keep his teeth from lengthening once again. The sane part of his brain warned that to drink from her again this soon would endanger her life. No matter how tempted he was to make her his permanent companion at the moment, he refused to be selfish. Several times in the past he'd been tempted to change a lover, but in the end had been glad he refrained. And for some reason, he didn't want to change her without her knowledge—or consent. But now was not the time to dwell on those thoughts.

Willow moaned again as he began to thrust inside of her, stopping any more thoughts from entering his mind. She reached one hand behind her to dig her nails into his hip, encouraging him.

He continued thrusting with deep, patient strokes he knew were driving her wild. He moved one hand to tease her breast for a moment before lowering it and playing with her clit, rubbing tight circles around it as he enjoyed the increase in her moans.

Still stroking her, he increased the speed of his thrusts to match the rhythm of his fingers. Willow's breath caught, and she let out a deep moan. He gave in to temptation. Gently biting the curve of her shoulder, he was careful not to allow his teeth to lengthen.

Her body tightened around him and he pinched her clit, tugging it between his thumb and forefinger, sending her over the edge. She shouted out his name and God's as her entire body trembled around him. Growling into her flesh, he was helpless as her pussy's milking contractions again tore away his control.

He held her in his tight embrace, still buried deep within her until she was fast asleep. Leaving her only long enough to grab the blankets and wrap them up, he returned to her, pulling her back into his arms.

Settling down, Seth rested his face close to her hair and breathed deeply, memorizing the smell of her. As he fell into the deep sleep of his kind, he was certain that she would rest until later that night without any "help" from him. Especially since he had fed off her a second time.

Chapter Four

Cracking her eyes open, Willow couldn't see much of anything around her. The room was cloaked completely in darkness. For a few moments, she felt disoriented. The sheets surrounding her didn't feel like the cotton set she'd put on her bed before she went to the bar with Roxy. They felt smooth and silky and she knew she didn't have any sheets like that. For a second she couldn't remember where she was. As her memory, and all the things she'd done with Seth, returned, her face began to flame.

"Good evening. I was beginning to worry. How do you feel?" The bed shifted slightly as Seth sat beside her.

"I'm fine, I think. A bit sore, but that's alright. And I'm starving." She chuckled as her stomach started to growl noisily. "What time is it?" She struggled to sit up in the bed, almost forgetting at first that she was naked under the sheets.

"Almost midnight. What would you like to eat?" With a click, Seth turned on a lamp located on one of the nightstands.

Her eyes closed instantly as the room suddenly became brighter. Cracking her eyes again, she let them adjust to the change before opening them fully. He sat patiently, a smile on his face, looking delicious in his casual attire. Once again she couldn't believe her luck. Had she really gotten to spend all night—and day—in his arms? Despite the slight distance separating them, she could practically feel the heat from his naked body as he pressed her deeper into the mattress when his hips thrust into her.

"I don't care, I'm pretty easy," she said absently, growing lost in her lustful thoughts. When she realized what she'd said, her embarrassment grew. "What I mean—what I meant to say is that I—I like just about every... Anything would be fine, thank you," she finally stammered out.

"How's pizza?" He smiled.

"That would be great."

"What would you like on it?"

"Mushrooms, pepperoni and tomatoes. Thank you." Seth began to stand. "Wait." She reached for him before he could move from the bed. Clinging to the sheet so it covered her naked flesh, she added, "Would you order some breadsticks for me too?"

"Sure. I'll be back in just a moment." Moving fluidly, Seth stood and exited the room.

Willow took a deep breath, trying to calm her nerves. She wasn't in high school anymore, but for some reason he made her feel like she was. Not in a bad way, but in the good, anxious to see him, nervous and hoping he wouldn't realize what a geek she was kind of way. Taking another deep breath, part of her was glad he didn't have a phone in his bedroom. She couldn't imagine how horrible it would have been if the ringing had interrupted them. But on the other hand, if he did, his friend could have called before just busting in and interrupting them. Her hand moved to her neck. Her eyes closed dreamily as she remembered the feeling of him sucking on her. And of course, she was sorry he'd had to leave the room to order her food. She wouldn't have minded being able to watch him, to listen to him talk a little longer.

Falling back against the bed, Willow couldn't believe how weak she felt. *Of course,* she reasoned, *having had fabulous sex and sleeping for twenty-four hours with no food in between would probably do that to a girl. Especially when that man is Seth!* She was still amazed at how energetic a lover he'd been. More than any other lover she'd ever had before him. He'd mastered her body, made her scream and beg for more. Never before had she ever had so much sex that her entire body felt stiff. But most importantly, she didn't care. She was still somehow ready for more. No matter how sore she was, it didn't stop the cravings to feel him over her, beneath her, behind her. In any position so long as his cock was buried within her.

Seth came back into the room, as though conjured by her thoughts. When he sat on the bed beside her once again, Willow's limbs felt even weaker by his nearness.

"I'm sorry that I didn't realize you were hungry earlier," he apologized.

"It's alright," she assured him. And she meant it. *I would gladly give up food for another day and night filled with wild, hot sex with you anytime.* Her stomach growled with hunger as her body starved for another taste of him. *Is he addictive?*

Who cares, that's one addiction I could definitely get used to!

Seth chuckled and the sound made her wet instantly.

"What's so funny?" She tried to control her body's desire, tried to keep herself from simply tackling him and having her way with him yet again.

"You looked so serious for a minute. I'm sorry." He tried to contain his smile.

"Do you mind if I shower before the pizza gets here?" With any luck, the hot water—or maybe she should use cold?—would relax her muscles and give her enough time to get a grip on her raging hormones.

"Not at all. There's a shower through there, the door just to your left." He pointed at the door as he spoke. "I'll get you a towel, and something to wear if you don't mind borrowing my clothes for a little while."

"That would be nice." The inner teenager he'd brought to life in her sighed as she thought about wearing his clothes, being able to smell him surrounding her.

Willow slowly began to rearrange herself, discovering she would be unable to continue to cover her body with the sheet when she stood. Seth was still sitting on the bed, and looked like he wasn't in any rush to get up. If anything, she thought she saw a challenging gleam his eyes. She decided it didn't matter if she walked the small distance naked. It wasn't as though he hadn't seen every inch of her body during their short time together. Hell, he'd seen so much more.

Releasing the material, she stretched before standing, and gathered her courage. When she was halfway across the room Willow looked over her shoulder. She saw Seth devouring her every movement. Nervousness flooded her and she tried to continue walking to the bathroom casually.

What does it matter if he's watching me? Taking a deep breath, she reminded herself it wasn't a big deal, that there was no reason to be nervous. He'd seen her do things no other man ever had. But for some reason it didn't calm her down. *Get it together. It's not like you didn't just spend the last day naked in his bed, doing sinfully wonderful things with him,* she scolded herself.

Releasing the breath she hadn't been aware she was holding, she closed the bathroom door behind her. Ignoring everything but the shower, she turned on the hot water and allowed it to warm while she relieved the sudden pressure on her bladder.

Looking around, she smiled. This was definitely the bathroom of a bachelor. Done in dark earth tones, it was neither cold nor sterile. Warm and inviting, it reflected Seth well. Standing, she completely resisted the urge to snoop and opened the opaque glass door, becoming enveloped by a spray of relaxing hot water. She let it run over her body, soothing the stiffness of her limbs for a few minutes. Using his shampoo, she washed her hair, hoping it wouldn't be too horrible to brush since he didn't seem to have any conditioner. Soap in hand, she was just about to wash her body when the bar was taken from her.

"Allow me." Seth's hungry gaze traveled the length of her.

Willow froze, surprised that she hadn't heard him open the door, but dismissed it easily, telling herself it was only because her head had been under the water. After a brief pause, she presented him with her back, her hands holding her hair up and out of his way. It took an enormous amount of control not to moan and melt beneath his hands. Slick with soap, he made sure to cover every inch of her back, stroking her body, massaging her muscles slightly. As he washed her legs, Willow wanted to scream. She felt certain that if he continued much longer she would fall flat on her ass because her bones had once again turned into jelly.

"Turn around," he commanded gently.

Willow obeyed instantly. He was kneeling beside her, uncaring of the water splashing onto his dark clothes, molding them tight to his body. With a gentle touch, he worked his way up one leg, then the other. Closing her eyes, she lost herself in his touch, but she was jerked back to reality when she flinched as he glided his soapy hand over the crease of one thigh. His eyes were apologetic as he looked up into her face.

"I'm alright," she assured him. *Please, please continue to wash me,* she begged in her mind. This was probably the most sensual shower she had ever had. When this thing between them ended, she wanted to have as many memories as she could stored for future reference—for future fantasies. She knew she'd never again be able to step into the shower without remembering this fantasy that he had turned into a reality for her.

Willow mentally shook her head. Logic told her that she should be finished; her thoughts and body should be overloaded from sex. She had already experienced more with Seth—more pleasure, more passion, more ecstasy, more orgasms—than she had with any other lover from her past. He was much more generous than any other man she'd met. The amazing thing was, he'd given her so much, and she'd only known him for one day.

Seth paused for a moment then continued lathering her body. Skipping over her mound, instead he moved straight to the slight curve of her stomach.

She'd long ago forgotten how much time she'd spent lamenting about that section of her body. Of her seemingly constant wish that she had a flat stomach. She had tried everything she could think of short of surgery, but nothing seemed to work. Her body was determined to hold on to the little bit of extra weight. But here, at this moment, with his hands gliding over her skin almost reverently, she lost the wish. She couldn't remember why it bothered her so much, why she saw it as such an imperfection. If this man, who oozed sex appeal from his every pore, didn't seem to care, why should she? He didn't seem to even notice the perceived flaw.

He continued moving up her body, skipping her breasts the way he had her mound, washing her neck, her arms, even her hands. He continued the gentle, erotic massage. Practically finished, he smiled up at her and lathered his hands generously.

Finally he began to wash her breasts, causing a moan to escape from her. He teased her nipples into becoming hard, tight buds for him. Slowly, making certain not even a single speck of dirt could have possibly escaped his notice, that no part of her breasts remained untouched, his hands moved lower.

Closing her eyes, Willow barely felt the hot spray still pouring down her back and neck as Seth ran one soapy finger across the folds of her sex. She only hoped that the small rivers running down her body masked exactly how wet she was for him at the moment. It was a little embarrassing the way her body reacted to his slightest touch. The way he seemed to make her want to moan and writhe, begging him to fill her. It was disconcerting that he had so much power over her body's reaction to him.

He stroked his fingers over her clit, dismissing any doubts she had that he didn't know precisely what he did to her. Cleaning her thoroughly, Seth made sure to continue his sensual attack on her. Standing, he ignored the water and suds splashing on him and removed the showerhead from its base. Positioning the spray between her legs, he focused it on her clit, letting the almost throbbing pulse of water bring her closer to orgasm. Backing against the wall so she wouldn't hurt herself if her muscles did crumble beneath her, Willow spread her legs farther apart, screaming with pleasure when his fingers entered her, as the spray continued to work its magic. Within seconds she was gripping his shoulders, crying out as yet another orgasm shot through her body.

Looking down at her, he licked his lips and leaned in as though he wanted to do much more, as though he wanted to finish what they had begun. Unfortunately, just outside the shower, a phone began to ring.

"I'd better go answer that." Regret filled his voice. "It should be the pizza." Giving her one final, lingering glance, he removed his fingers from her body and replaced the showerhead before stepping out of the spraying water.

When he was gone, Willow cursed modern conveniences, wishing she had gone hungry instead of getting him to order pizza, because at least then he would still be in the shower with her.

With Seth gone, the shower no longer held any appeal for her. After his caresses, the water no longer felt as hot and relaxing; it was no longer soothing. Instead, it simply made her want to race through his apartment and drag him back in there to join her. As she turned the water off, Willow wondered if a shower would ever feel as good to her again—especially without him there to tease her. Opening the glass door, she saw a large, fluffy white towel hanging up, waiting for her. Beside it she saw a green tee shirt and nothing else.

Holding the towel, she almost dropped it when she gripped her stomach, willing it to behave for just a few more minutes when she caught a whiff of the pizza and breadsticks. It gave a loud protest while she dried herself as quickly as she could. Her sensitive body flinched when she pressed the soft towel against certain areas. When she was mostly dry, she grabbed the shirt and pulled it over her head. It ended at the top of her thighs, only barely covering her pussy and again, Willow had to remind herself not to feel embarrassed. The memory of his erotic washing, combined with her stomach's growling, forced her to dismiss any possible awkwardness and begin working on her hair. Grunting through the tangles, she brushed her hair as fast as she could. When she was satisfied and decided she was presentable—that her long hair was as tame as it was going to get—she walked out of the bathroom.

In the bedroom she avoided looking at the rumpled bed as she allowed her nose to guide her to the food. Walking through the hallway, she was amazed by just how much she had missed, just how distracted she'd been when he carried her through his apartment the previous night.

Leaving the hallway, she was surprised to see the elevator opened directly into his home. She hadn't believed his apartment was quite so generous. *Of course, until now, I've only seen the hallway, his bedroom and master bath...*

"Wow," she said aloud, looking around at the beautiful furnishings as she passed. The main room, the one directly in front of the elevator, was so large it had been divided in half. To the left there was a large formal living room, filled with expensive furniture she wasn't sure weren't antiques.

To the right, a giant portrait of a beautiful sunset filled with pinks and oranges, hung above a marble fireplace in the cozy area. This part was filled with furniture that looked incredibly comfortable. It was the kind of furniture that inspired thoughts of cuddling beside the fireplace and just snuggling as the flames glowed. There was a recliner just off to the side, she noticed with a smile. Her mind instantly turned to some of the more interesting things she could do with Seth while he was sitting in the chair.

Her stomach gave another low growl and, looking around, she wondered where exactly he could be hiding the kitchen. Following her nose wouldn't work any longer. The large room seemed to be filled with the tempting aroma.

"Over here," Seth called to her, sticking his head around a corner just past the cozy area.

Willow followed him to find an amazing dining room, extravagantly decorated with a crystal chandelier hanging down over the center of a large dark table that could've fit twenty people around it, with room to spare. Looking at the beautiful fixture, she could imagine it throwing little rainbows all over the room when the sunlight hit it just right.

Sitting in front of the large pizza box, she opened it, her stomach once again grumbling at being neglected for so long. Without a single thought to modesty, she picked up two of the biggest slices she saw and put them on a plate. Opening the package of breadsticks sitting beside the box, she grabbed one and tore a bite out of it, her eyes drifting shut with pleasure.

"Would you like something to drink?"

"Water's fine, thanks." As soon as she swallowed the food in her mouth, she began to devour the pizza. She couldn't believe how hungry she felt, how heavenly the pizza tasted. Looking at the box, she could almost believe she'd be able to eat the entire meal all by herself.

Seth brought her a glass filled with water then sat across from her.

"I'm sorry, I don't mean to be such a pig. My mom would die if she saw my manners. Would you like some?"

"No. I enjoyed something earlier, but thank you." He had a strange look on his face that she couldn't quite read. But since it didn't make her feel like he was some homicidal maniac about to kill her, she contentedly continued to eat.

After eating another slice of pizza and two more breadsticks, she forced herself to stop. She didn't want to make herself sick by eating too much or too fast.

For a moment they sat in companionable silence, both just content to simply relax. From somewhere in the apartment she heard a clock strike the hour and jumped from the shock as the bell echoed in the silence.

"Is it really that late? Where did the time go?"

"You know what they say, time flies when you're having fun." He smiled seductively.

Willow blushed again at the gleam in his eyes. He looked as though he wanted to devour her, much like she had the pizza. Her pussy flooded, and she was again astonished by how he could make her incredibly wet, so ready with just a look.

"May I use your phone?" she asked suddenly, trying to break the spell he had cast over her body.

"Of course."

Seth led her to a small cordless phone set up in the less formal area of his living room. It was the section that Jason had persuaded him into creating. He was much more comfortable on the other side, among the items that reminded him of his youth, or other pleasant times in his life. There wasn't a single piece of furniture in the more formal room, not a single piece of bric-a-brac, that didn't hold a fond memory for him. Jason had tried to entice him to sell some of his collection once, but he could not be persuaded to part with the items, no matter how generous an offer was made.

Looking at Willow, however, he was glad he had caved in and created the less formal area as well. He was about to leave, to allow her some privacy when she stopped him by placing her hand on his arm. Sitting beside her on the overstuffed couch, he was careful not to touch her. He knew if he did, he would pull her into his arms. From there he would kiss her, and, especially after the shower he had given her, he felt sure things would escalate until he was buried within her again. Sometimes modern conveniences were most inconvenient in his opinion.

From his position beside her, he could smell her arousal. That tempted him more than the thought of tasting her blood. He could barely resist tasting her blood flowing into his mouth. He knew if he touched her he wouldn't be able to resist tasting her sweet cream on his tongue again. Never before had any woman been so tempting to all of his senses, so addictive.

"Hello? Roxy, it's Willow. No, no, calm down, I'm fine. I just didn't realize it had gotten quite this late." She paused as the person on the other end, Roxy, spoke. "Yes, I'm sure you guys were worried about me, but I'm fine." Another pause. "Yes...hold on."

"Um, where are we?" Willow blushed prettily as she covered the mouthpiece and admitted she wasn't sure where she was.

He smiled, unable to blame the girl for not paying more attention to her surroundings the previous night. They both had other, more pressing, things on their minds.

"Is there a problem?"

"No, it's just—in order for my friends to come pick me up I need to be able to tell them where I am," she explained.

"I'd be happy to take you wherever you want to go."

For a minute she just sat and stared at him.

He decided to take a chance. "If you don't have any other plans, somewhere else you have to be, you are welcome to stay here. We could talk or..." His voice trailed off, allowing her imagination to run wild with all the possibilities. He tried to keep his expression neutral, though inside he prayed she would stay with him longer.

"Roxy, I think I'm going to stay here a little longer... No, Seth will bring me back home... Yes, I know... I'll be fine... Well, it's not like I have something to do... Look." Willow sighed. "I'm a big girl... Yes, I know I'm your little sister, but that's not the point. I'll be fine. I'll call you, okay... Yeah, alright...bye." She hit the end button, looking uncertain of her decision now that the call was over.

"Is everything all right?" Seth wished he could think of something better to say. He felt like a fool, but again refused to go snooping through her brain. Typically it didn't bother him to find out what he wanted to know regardless, but with her it was different.

"It's fine. My sister just worries about me. I've... Well, I've never just disappeared with a strange guy before. That combined with the craziness that's been going on the last few days have made her worry more than usual. When she didn't hear from me earlier, I guess she just started to freak."

"That's understandable. But I promise you'll come to no harm while you are here. I am glad to hear you don't typically go home with just any man, though." He was more relieved than he should be, but pushed those thoughts to the side.

"Thanks." She looked around the room. "What do we do now?"

Seth laughed, his head falling backward for a second as the amusement bubbled out of him. She seemed so innocent at times.

"We can do whatever you want to do, sweetheart." He gave her a molten look. He knew what activities he would enjoy, but would put no pressure on her.

"I wouldn't mind watching a movie or something but I haven't seen a TV anywhere..." Her voice trailed off as she looked around the room.

"I don't watch much television." It was the truth. He was about to show her where the large television that Jason had also talked him into installing was hidden, but she spoke.

"Oh. Well then, what would you suggest we do?" She blushed as she glanced at him and saw how he was looking at her. He knew he had to be devouring her with his gaze. "Why don't we talk," she suggested.

"Talk?"

"Yeah, talk. I'm going to be honest with you. More honest than I've been with most guys I've ever been with, especially after just meeting them." Her face turned a delicate shade of pink. "I want you. I really, *really* want to feel you inside me again. But I'm not used to being just a...a sex toy. This is all new to me and I don't want to overstay my welcome."

"As I said before, you are welcome to stay as long as you like." His voice was low and husky. Despite his intentions, it was hard to try to control the lust filling him. "But if you wish to talk, then we shall talk."

"What's your favorite color?" She burst into a fit of giggles when the question was out. "I'm sorry, this just feels really weird. Usually the silly questions come before the wild, uninhibited sex."

He lifted her hand and kissed the back, his tongue lingering on her skin. "My favorite color is burgundy."

"I think you are the first person I've ever met who picked that color."

Seth shrugged. "What kind of crazy stuff has been going on that would make your sister worry?"

Willow nibbled her lip gently. He easily read her reluctance to "spill her guts" as she had phrased it on her face. He was learning her mannerisms and since he was fairly certain she wasn't about to throw her head back and scream with pleasure, the nibbling on her lip must mean she was nervous.

"Just this jerk I work—used to work with," she corrected herself.

"What happened?" He shifted on the couch, hoping his expression portrayed his genuine interest.

"Basically, he told me if I didn't sleep with him he would spread rumors around the office that we humped like bunnies. I didn't believe him. And the company didn't believe me." She rolled her eyes. "They said I was trying to screw my way to the top and they would not have me tarnishing their good name."

"Why would they believe him instead of you?"

"He was my boss," she confessed quietly. "A complete jerk who took credit for my ideas and my work. I didn't really mind that part. But I hated the way he looked at me. Like he wanted to gobble me up or something." Willow shook her head. "It made me feel like I had bugs crawling all over my flesh." Willow shuddered.

Turning his head, Seth felt guilty. He hadn't realized he was making her uncomfortable with his desire. He knew he looked at her hungrily, could feel his every cell begging to touch her again.

"I'm sorry if I made you uncomfortable." He spoke without looking at her. He hadn't meant to make her consider him a lecherous rogue.

"I didn't mean..." Willow sighed. "I like the way *you* look at me," she confessed. "More than I should, to be honest. With you I get more of a tingly feeling." She waited until he looked at her again. Surprising him, she took his hand in her own. "The tingles start here." She placed his hand on her stomach. "Then spread up here." She brought his hand up to cup her breast, hissing from pleasure when his thumb brushed against her nipple, causing it to grow firm. "And down here." She guided his hand lower on her body and beneath the hem of her borrowed shirt, down to where she was already dripping for him.

As his fingers lightly brushed against her, she didn't care if she was just his temporary girl toy. She wanted—no, she needed to feel his hands on her, feel him inside of her. Moving his hand much as he had done with hers, she separated one finger from the rest and lifted his hand to her mouth, sucking the digit into her mouth.

"Just sitting here, trying to hold a simple conversation with you is hard. I can't think of anything to say with my body screaming like it is, for you." Guiding his moist finger from her mouth, she positioned it at the wet entrance to her pussy. "You've barely touched me and I already want you." She moaned softly as he allowed her to slide his finger into her passage. "I'm already wet for you."

"I thought you wanted to take a break." His voice was low, quiet. He sounded almost hypnotized by her voice, her movements.

Willow smiled slowly as she pushed his hand away. Climbing off the incredibly comfortable couch, she lowered to her knees between his legs. Looking up into his eyes, she tried to gauge his reaction as she unfastened his jeans and lowered the zipper carefully. As soon as his already semi-erect cock came into view, she leaned down to it. Taking the velvety tip between her lips, she swirled her tongue around it. Teasing the small hole on top she then opened her mouth wider, sucking in his entire length. After a few strokes of her mouth, he was fully erect between her lips.

But she didn't stop. The night before she had been denied the pleasure of feeling him inside her mouth the way she'd wanted and wouldn't deny herself the pleasure now. She continued to suck his cock, not attempting to hide the moans of pleasure coming from her throat. His hands wrapped in her hair and he pulled her, pouting, from her feast. Before she had a chance to complain, she let out a long moan as he settled her onto his lap, his hard cock sliding easily into her hungry pussy as he kissed her deeply.

Rocking her hips, she lifted off him, until only the tip remained inside of her before lowering herself onto him again. The slow pace she set was driving her wild, but she wanted to take her time, wanted to enjoy every minute, every single inch of him as he moved within her.

Seth shifted slightly, placing his hand between their bodies to circle her clit. Throwing her head back, she matched the pace of her thrusts with the hand stroking her. Deep inside, her orgasm built until she was grinding her hips against his cock and hand as hard as she could.

As she came, she saw stars of every color bursting beneath her closed eyelids. He shifted his hand, releasing her to pull her harder still against him and, after a few short strokes, he growled out his pleasure, and she knew he had joined her in the heavens.

Chapter Five

"By the old gods, I like the way you talk."

"That wasn't quite what I had in mind when I made the suggestion. But it felt really, really good." Willow chuckled, her head resting on Seth's shoulder. Beneath her, he was still almost completely dressed as she sat on his lap with his cock buried inside her. "I just hope you don't want to get up anytime soon."

His chest rumbled from his deep laughter. When he finally got his amusement under control he pressed a kiss to her neck, clenching his jaw shut to keep himself from drinking from her yet again. *It's too soon for that,* he reminded himself.

"And don't think I didn't notice the marks, buddy. No one has ever given me a hickey on my leg before. That is definitely going to be hard to explain."

"And why would people be asking questions? Why would anyone see it?" The thought of anyone else seeing her naked body sprawled before them hit him, sparking his anger. His teeth threatened to lengthen and rip said person limb from limb.

"Well, what if I decide I want to go swimming? I don't wear a grandma bathing suit you know."

It was as if she flipped some kind of switch. With those simple words she'd eased his anger. "What kind do you wear?" He stroked her back, his fingers lingering on her bare ass.

"You tell me," she said with a smile. "What do you think I wear?"

Closing his eyes, he concentrated only on her bathing suit. An image appeared to him, so vivid and erotic his cock stirred to life once again. "A bikini. Not quite a string bikini, but very alluring. One that is modest enough so you don't feel naked and exposed, but small enough to drive any man crazy at the sight of you in it."

"I don't know if I've heard it described that way before, but that's close." Her tone turned somber. "Really close. How did you know?"

Smiling, he avoided the question since he refused to lie to her. Instead he distracted her by tilting his head and stroking the edge of her ear with his tongue before sucking her lobe into his mouth.

"Wow, that feels really good." Her voice was muffled as she pressed her nose to his neck. Opening her mouth, she gently nipped his flesh before placing a tender kiss on the same spot. His cock grew harder.

Willow groaned, lifting herself off him. He wanted to pull her back, to thrust deep inside her again, but allowed her to have her space.

"I'm sorry, I know I'm giving you mixed signals. This is all just so new to me." His pride was salved by the sadness in her voice as she sat beside him, resting her head on his shoulder again.

"You mentioned a movie earlier, why don't we go out and see one?" He made the suggestion, hoping a more public place would help him to control himself. That it would be able to help him manage this almost desperate need he seemed to have to touch her, be buried deep inside her...

"Are you sure? I don't want to keep you from anything..."

"I'm sure." He smiled. Would he ever get enough of the shy girl that appeared when the brazen lover was sated?

"That would be nice. But..." She hesitated.

"But," he prompted.

"I don't really have anything to wear. I'm not even sure where the clothes I wore here are..." Her voice trailed off as her cheeks blossomed in embarrassment.

He smiled at the memory of him throwing her clothes all over his bedroom in his hurry to feel her naked in his arms.

"I guess I could just borrow one of your shirts... Maybe just pretend it was a shirt dress?" She made the suggestion quickly, as though she was trying to convince herself it would be acceptable. As Willow stood, her face turned a darker shade of red. "I'm sorry about your couch..."

In one fluid motion he stood, fixing his own clothes. Joining her, he followed her gaze to the damp spot she'd left where some of their fluids had leaked from her body.

"Don't be. Lucky couch," he growled, kissing her again. Pulling back while he was still able to, Seth took her hand and led her to his bedroom to get her a different shirt.

In practically no time they were standing in line for popcorn. The jacket Seth had loaned her for their ride to the theater was slung casually over his forearm. As they waited their turn, Willow felt comforted having Seth stand beside her. His arm was wrapped protectively around her waist. The action, combined with the visible mark on her neck, made her certain that anyone who cared to look would know instantly she was with him. But even the knowledge that Seth would protect her didn't stop the blushes she felt as guys stared appreciatively at her body. For Willow, it was a little unnerving to be out wearing only one of her lover's shirts and her heels.

Thankfully the second shirt he'd given her that night ended mid-thigh instead of barely below her pussy. Still, the knowledge that she wasn't wearing any underwear underneath made her tingle with anticipation, with pleasure, knowing that she was doing something naughty.

Not for the first time since she'd climbed off his lap, she cursed her body. She'd love nothing more than to continue the sex-a-thon they'd been having back at his apartment, but she had to face facts. And the simple fact was she'd had more sex with him in the last two nights than she'd had in the last six months. And the night wasn't finished yet. Her body was pleasantly sore all over. And with every step she took she was aware of the mark he had put on her upper thigh, in the crease of her leg. She still didn't understand why he put one there. *But I won't press him about it. Not that it would do any good,* she thought grumpily.

When it was their turn, Willow ordered popcorn with extra butter and a large soda. She really shouldn't be hungry after all the pizza she had eaten, but for some reason she couldn't seem to feel quite full. Maybe it was the unexpected sex on his couch that brought her appetite back.

When the clerk asked what he wanted, Seth replied, "Nothing, thank you," then paid for Willow's refreshments.

She waited until they were seated near the back of the theater before she asked him about it. "Why didn't you get anything?"

Blood rushed to her face when he gave an appreciative look at the long expanse of thigh revealed as the shirt rose when she sat, almost exposing the golden curls covering her mound. Thankfully he sat to her right and the wall was to her left. They were in the back of the theater and were attending a late enough show that she didn't believe anyone would be so close to them that they would notice her nakedness. She was just about to comment on his glance when a couple walked down the row toward them.

Once the girlfriend got a look at her though, she tugged her man backward until they were as far from Willow as possible. Neither she nor Seth tried to suppress their laughter.

"Would you like to share my popcorn?" She asked the question just to have something to say.

"I don't snack much."

"Oh come on, you can't come to the movies and not eat popcorn. Besides, for some reason it tastes really good tonight. Just the right amount of extra butter and salt..." She picked a piece of popcorn up and presented it to him.

Seth lowered his head and took her offering, a shiver of delight racing down her back and straight to her pussy as he made certain to suck the butter from her fingertip.

"Delicious," he commented. She was almost positive he wasn't talking about the popcorn.

The theater grew darker and the few people scattered through the room grew quiet, waiting for the show. As the previews began, Seth laid his hand on her leg, near her knee. She ached for him to touch her more, wishing for just a moment that she could make up her mind. Either she wanted to be his sex toy, or she wanted something similar to a normal date, even if it hadn't been called one. The constant swinging back and forth making her grumpy, but at the moment she decided she wouldn't question it. However long she had with him, she was determined to enjoy every moment of it. And that included feeling the not unpleasant ache that said her body had been well sated several times.

Feeling wonderfully young and wicked, Willow decided she wanted to play. She had always been good in public. She was the only girl she knew who had never made out at the movies. This was too good a chance to pass up. *After all, how many times in my life will I be out with a drop-dead gorgeous man, wearing only his shirt?*

Seth had already done amazing things to her, things she hadn't believed possible. Just being around him made her want to try new things—experiences that had never appealed to her before. He made her bold, adventurous. But would he go along with it? There was only one way to find out.

She shifted, opening her legs slightly and, laying her hand on top his, nudged it a little higher. She moved it until it rested about halfway up her thigh. She took it as a good sign when he didn't pull his hand away after a couple of previews. Unfortunately, he hadn't taken the hint either.

Gathering her courage, Willow nudged his hand higher still, to the edge of the shirt, no more than an inch away from her mound, which now seemed to be begging for his touch. Again, she waited to see how he would react and once again he left his hand exactly where she had placed it.

It's now or never, she told herself as the theater darkened more and the movie began. Closing the distance between his hand and her sensitive clit, she smiled at how wet she already was, just from the thought of being naughty in public with him, where they could be caught at any minute. Moving her hand off his once it was in position, she placed it on the growing bulge in his jeans, stroking his cock through the material.

Beside her, Seth shifted slightly and she felt disappointed that he wasn't feeling adventurous at the moment. He removed her hand from his hard cock and gathered up the light jacket he'd loaned her for the ride over from the seat beside him. With care he arranged it on her lap, as though she were cold. Turning to ask him about it, she quieted when he slid his hand beneath the covering, nudging her thighs apart. She willingly spread them, allowing his hand better access to her dripping pussy.

Willow bit her lip as he stroked his fingers up and down her folds, before parting them to play with her clit. Much more of his torture and anyone who entered the theater after they left would believe the previous occupant had had an "accident" in the seat.

Squirming, she chanced a look at him. His face was impassive as he watched the movie, giving no indication of exactly what he was doing to her. Looking at her, he gave a mischievous wink, a smile tilting his lips a second before he leaned in to give her a lingering kiss. His talented fingers brought her close to orgasm time and again, always stopping just short, winding the tension in her body tighter and tighter.

Halfway through the movie, Seth huffed, shaking his head. Grunting and mumbling something about the movie that she couldn't quite understand, he left his seat. Before she could move, he spread her legs wider, kneeling between them. One minute she was looking down at him in confusion, the next his head was covered by the jacket, his tongue replacing the finger on her clit.

Moaning, Willow shoved her knuckle inside her mouth when someone turned their head and heatedly whispered "shhhh". She pretended to watch the screen along with everyone else.

At his urging, she shifted in her seat, slouching lower, her pussy sliding to the edge of the seat. Beneath the jacket, he draped her legs over his shoulders, rewarding her cooperation by sliding a finger into her dripping hole. Again she bit down on her knuckle to prevent herself from making a sound.

As the climactic fight in the movie unfolded, he added another finger and sped up his thrusting as he suckled her clit. Her body seemed to tune in with the movie. The closer it got to the end of the scene, the closer her orgasm approached. Unable to fight it any longer, Willow clenched her legs together. Her thighs gripped his head, her ankles pressed into his back as she allowed one hand beneath the jacket to grip a handful of his hair. She urged him closer, grinding her hips harder against his face. His tongue entered her, and she felt him lapping at the cream flowing freely from her body.

Her legs were trembling with the force of her orgasm as Willow bit down on her finger so hard she soon had the coppery taste of her own blood in her mouth to keep from screaming out.

Seth waited for her body to stop clenching, her thighs to relax before he discreetly returned to his seat, a grin of pure masculine pride on his face as he licked the corners of his mouth. As she watched, he grabbed one of the napkins she'd gotten for the popcorn and wiped his chin.

They remained seated as the credits rolled and the lights were raised, waiting for their fellow audience members to leave and her limbs to be strong enough to carry her weight. When she was ready, he gathered the jacket and helped her put it back on. His arm curved around her waist, and with his help, she managed to step away without stumbling. Though she was curious, Willow refused to look back at her seat. She didn't want her face to redden or show any signs of guilt at how large the wet spot she'd left had to be.

Climbing carefully onto his motorcycle behind him, Willow was reminded again of her near nakedness. In front of her, Seth's ass pressed intimately against her. The motor vibrated beneath her, making her thankful that she'd just had such a strong orgasm. Otherwise—after all the teasing he had done to her—they would never have made it back to his home in one piece. The hum of the engine against her body would have had her stroking him, enticing him to satisfy her rather than concentrate on the road.

Neither spoke until they were once again safely in the elevator, on their way up to his home.

"What happened to your finger?" Seth's voice was full of concern as he looked at the wound hanging by her side.

"Oh, that... Well, I couldn't exactly make much noise in public, could I?" She enjoyed teasing him. She felt like she'd been doing it forever. "It'll be fine. It was well worth it," she admitted, briefly wondering if it was a mistake to reveal so much to him.

"I'm glad you enjoyed yourself." The mischievous grin was back on his face.

Willow laughed. "Yeah, well, would you mind telling me about the movie we just saw? 'Cause I didn't catch one blessed scene after the title."

"You didn't miss much. It amazes me how many movies Hollywood releases portray vampires as being evil, power-hungry individuals who are hell-bent on destroying the world."

"You don't think they are?"

"I believe they are like every other living creature. There are those who deserve to have the reputation of a monster and those who simply wish to be left alone to live in peace."

"I always thought they were, you know, not living."

"Why? Because movies always claim that is the way of things?"

"Well, yeah. I mean, we are talking about fictional characters aren't we?" Her mood turned serious.

He was saved from having to reply when the doors opened, but Willow couldn't help wondering how he would have answered her last question. She berated herself as being silly. *Of course vampires aren't real.*

She let him lead her straight to the kitchen. "Allow me to bandage it for you." He placed a finger against her lips when she tried to object. "It's the least I can do for causing such a wound."

"Funny," she mockingly scolded him, still feeling too playful to be truly upset. "You don't seem the least bit remorseful." She jumped up to sit on the countertop as he pulled out a first-aid kit. "Isn't it funny how much things change?" She closed her eyes and mused aloud. "When you're a kid all you need is someone to kiss a wound, and it's all better." Opening her eyes, she stared into his deep blue gaze and felt almost spellbound.

Smiling, he stopped fiddling with the now rarely used first-aid kit that was only in the apartment because of Jason. For once he was glad that the other man had been accident-prone as a child. Putting the small kit on the counter beside Willow, he lifted her finger to his lips.

He promised himself he would be good, that he would resist the temptation of her blood. He would simply kiss her wound then bandage it.

As her blood teased his lips, Seth's good intentions flew out the proverbial window. Taking her finger into his mouth, he lightly sucked on the wound. One razor sharp tooth instantly reversed her clotting and allowing her blood to mix with the lingering traces of her cream on his tongue. The combination made his cock rock hard instantly.

Allowing himself only a few precious seconds to taste her, he swiped his tongue over the wound again, only allowing it to clot. Carefully he made certain not to close the wound fully, knowing she would become suspicious if it were to be suddenly, miraculously healed. The scent of her arousal served to make his desire more urgent.

He finally pulled her finger out of his mouth. "All better?"

"What?" She looked dazed.

"Your finger, is it better now that it got a kiss?"

"My finger?" Her eyes were dark with passion. "Oh, my finger. Yeah, thanks." She licked her lips as she watched him place the small bandage around her wound.

"Tell me about yourself." He was trying to ease the sexual tension in the air. He didn't want her to think she was just a sex toy to him. But he also wasn't ready to delve into what that revelation could mean, or why it mattered to him. He only knew that he really did want to find out more about her.

"There isn't much to tell. My sister is pretty cool, but she can get overprotective."

"What brought you over to my table the other night? I'm not complaining, but I do wonder what possible explanation there could be for my amazing luck."

"I just... Well, I can't tell you. But I will tell you I am very glad I did come over."

For the first time since he'd met her, his curiosity won out. He knew it was wrong, but he couldn't resist the temptation yet again. Staring deeply into her eyes, he easily slipped into her mind, finding the memory he was looking for. Before his mind's eye, her day replayed for him. How her boss had looked at her. He understood now why she'd said her boss made her skin crawl when he stared at her that way. He saw the way her boss smirked as his supervisor fired her. His expression clearly saying better than words "you should have just slept with me". Seth fought off a growl as he resisted the urge to find this ass and teach him to show more respect for women.

Pressing forward, he "fast-forwarded" to when she was at the bar. He saw her sister look at her and announce her as the player in some game.

Guilt flooded him at gaining the knowledge in such a way. Breaking the stare, he saw her eyes were glazed, as though she were in a daze.

After a few seconds, Willow shook her head. "I'm sorry, I must have drifted off for a minute. What did you say?"

"Nothing important, sweetheart."

A look of regret washed over her face. "Oh, that's right, you asked about last night. Honestly, I'm not sure I'd even want to tell you why I walked over there if I could. It's embarrassing." She wouldn't look him in the eye.

"Really?"

"Well, see, I'm not supposed to tell you. And I really shouldn't, it doesn't speak well of me..."

"But?" He prompted her. He was trying to remain neutral, trying his best not to pressure her into answering if she really didn't want to. But he wanted to know what possible game she'd played.

"But I will if you want to know." She paused, as if waiting for him to say yes or no, still refusing to look him in the eye. After a moment she continued despite his silence. "My friends came up with this game. It's silly really. They were trying to make me feel better. You pick a guy and go ask him what kind of underwear he wears. If you guessed right, you can give him your number and a kiss. But commando is always rewarded with a full-on French kiss."

"I take it you guessed incorrectly?" He couldn't hide the smile in his voice. He hadn't delved that far into her thoughts and memories. Now he almost wished he had.

"No, I didn't." He arched an eyebrow as she continued her explanation. "You didn't exactly give me a chance to give you my number and leave," she explained.

"No, I didn't." He smiled, not attempting to sound sorry. "So, you only came over because of a game?" His pride was a little wounded when confronted with the fact. *But the important thing is* that *she did come over, not why,* he tried to tell himself.

Her blush gave him his answer.

"Oh, Seth, don't look like that." She sounded remorseful. "Yes, it's the reason I came over, but..." Her blush grew. "According to the rules, all I had to do was kiss you. Everything else...everything else was because I wanted to."

Looking into her eyes, he didn't need to probe her mind to discover she was telling the truth. Her emotions were right there for him to see. She was an open book.

"To be honest, I'm glad they talked me into playing. I'm not sure I'd have been brave enough to approach you on my own." Her hand reached up, cupping his cheek. "It was the only time I've ever played, and I told my sister I'm not playing again. I only did it because I was having a really bad day and I thought I could use a little fun. I'm really glad I agreed."

Taking her hand in his, he placed a lingering kiss on her palm. "So am I, sweetheart."

"What else is there to do so late at night?"

Seth allowed the change of subject. He wanted to take her back into the bedroom and give in to his thirst for her. Both for her body and her blood. *No,* he scolded himself. *I need to get her out in public, where I'll be able to better control myself.*

"We could go out dancing?"

"I'd like that. But are you sure I'm dressed appropriately? Being in a dark theater is one thing, but dancing..." Her voice trailed off.

"Sweetheart, I think you look amazing," he practically purred. His gaze caressed her scantily clad form and caused Willow to blush prettily for him.

Chapter Six

Stretching in the luxurious bed, it was hard to believe she'd been at Seth's home for almost a week now. She was careful to call her sister every few days to prevent the other woman from worrying too badly. Willow had to call her again that night, but she didn't want to. They always ended up arguing. Roxy couldn't understand why she stayed, why Willow wouldn't come home.

It's amazing, how used to sleeping all day and staying awake all night one can get. Willow finally climbed out of the bed and walked over to the windows, looking at the beautifully lit skyline.

On their way back to his apartment from the club they'd gone to after their titillating movie experience, she had made a comment that she should get a few things to wear in public if they were going to go out again.

She'd had every intention of going home and packing a few things to use at his home. Instead Seth surprised her the next night by taking her shopping. When she modeled the clothes for him in the store, he'd whispered in her ear how much he enjoyed watching her walk around his home wearing one of his shirts and nothing else. She was still blushing when he paid for the few outfits she had picked out.

After their trip to buy her clothes, he'd taken her to the grocery store, convincing her to fill the cart with foods she liked. She'd been stunned. His thoughtful gestures told her better than words could that he wanted her to stick around. It revealed how much he enjoyed having her in his home. He'd been so generous with her, she felt guilty, almost as though she were taking advantage of him. But any time she mentioned paying him back, he'd pull her into his arms and kiss her until she melted. Then he would smile and nibble on her shoulder.

Walking to where she'd placed her shirt for the night, Willow dressed in his favorite color, burgundy. More amazing to her was the fact that not only did he not care if she went through his closet or drawers to pick something out, he'd even made room for the items she'd begun to accumulate. In his shower, beside his shampoo, he'd surprised her one night when she woke up with her own bottles of shampoo and conditioner. Walking into the bathroom, she smiled at the gradual signs there was now a woman using the room. Her favorite fruit-scented lotion sat on his pristine counter near the brush he'd bought for her. His toothbrush now had a mate as well.

Stretching, she smiled before she began her attempt to tame her hair. Her muscles were getting much more limber, her body less stiff, and she couldn't be happier. She'd grown used to his daily massages with a wonderful oil, which always seemed to turn into foreplay.

I am definitely becoming spoiled, Willow thought with a smile, thinking back to his tender kisses and caresses. But he wasn't always gentle. When they fucked, he knew he drove her crazy whenever he pounded into her body, making her scream out in pleasure as she experienced orgasm after orgasm.

Once she finished brushing her hair, she walked out of the room and headed for the dining room, where she knew he would be waiting for her.

Seth watched her walk into the room and once again gave thanks that she was in his life. After her confession, he'd done much thinking about her answer. He decided it didn't matter what brought her over to his table, only that she had joined him.

As he waited for her to sit down, his conscience began to scold him yet again. Ever since she'd revealed her secret, he'd felt like an ass for deceiving her. Too many centuries had passed since he'd last been tempted to entrust a mortal with the truth about who he was. He felt certain Willow would want—*no, that isn't right,* he corrected, *she would feel she deserved to know I am a vampire.* Thus far she seemed content to only know what he was wiling to say, never pressing him if he didn't wish to discuss a subject. At least not since she asked those uncomfortable questions about why he had been sucking on her thigh. His conscience had begun to grow more insistent that he reveal the truth.

Staring at her as she proudly wore his favorite deep red shirt, his hunger swelled yet again. Despite the fact that she now had clothing in his apartment to wear, she'd consented to his request that she only wear his tops. Since the first time he'd drank from her, he'd been unable to slake his thirst with another. No one's blood tasted as sweet as hers, none satisfied him as completely—or at all it seemed—but he continued to drink from them, fearing harm would come to her if he didn't. And he'd long ago decided no harm would come to his woman. He wasn't exactly sure when she'd ceased to be Willow, a woman he was merely having fun with, to Willow, his woman. In the end, it didn't mater. As far as he was concerned, she *was* his woman now, and he didn't want to lose her.

And in a moment of honesty he admitted that was the real reason he hadn't told her the truth yet. Because he was afraid she would leave and he would never see her again. That she would think he was some crazy man, or someone looking for a free meal. Just the thought of never seeing her smile again made his chest become tight and caused his heart to ache.

"Wow, that looks delicious. I do believe you are trying to spoil me, sir."

Smiling, he seated Willow at the table then placed the fresh plate of linguine he'd ordered in front of her. He had completely forgotten about it as he looked at her, enjoying her beauty.

"It smells wonderful," she sighed, taking a deep breath.

Nodding, he agreed completely with her. Something did look delicious. But to him, it was her.

"It has been my pleasure to spoil you. You are very easy to please."

Willow blushed at his double entendre and his cock began to harden just thinking about tasting her the way he had all those nights ago. How it had been, letting the cream from her sweet pussy linger on his tongue as her blood blended perfectly to create the most intoxicating taste he'd ever experienced. His mouth watered as he thought of drinking the cream from her body then driving her over the edge by drinking from her upper thigh. It still amazed him how easily she'd found pleasure, how hard she'd orgasmed simply from his bite. He'd never known that to happen with another woman. At least, not without a little "help" from him.

He'd restrained his desire to taste her completely for almost a week. Five incredibly long nights had passed. Five nights filled with temptation. The temptation to drink her blood; to change her into his eternal mate. If he was careful, he believed it would be safe for him to drink from her again. His teeth lengthened as he thought about drinking from her with her consent, not having to hide what he did and being able to share his pleasure with her.

How would it feel to not have to hide behind smoke screens any longer? Would her blood become more intoxicating to him? Would she still accept him for who and what he was? Could he ever let her go if she didn't?

"Seth?"

Smiling, he forced back the serious thoughts. "Yes, sweetheart?"

"I asked if you were going to eat anything."

"I'm not hungry right now. I'll grab a quick bite later."

"Okay," she said and let the subject drop. The look on her face told him things were not okay. Willow was beginning to wonder about him, if the questions hadn't already begun.

An hour later they sat cuddling on the big, soft, comfortable couch by the phone while Willow spoke with her sister. It had become their ritual. When he tried to give her privacy, she stopped him. She told him she took comfort in feeling his arms around her as she argued with her sister.

Looking down, he couldn't help himself. He was drawn to her, felt as though an eternity had passed since he last tasted her. Watching her neck, he could see the vein there throbbing in time with her heartbeat. He could smell the lotion he'd grown to love all over her skin. Calling himself a weak fool, he acknowledged that he'd fed regularly to avoid this exact situation. But now, with her pressed so close, he felt as though he were starving and she were the only one who would—could—be able to satisfy his thirst.

Lowering his mouth to her neck, to the spot she loved for him to kiss and tease, he traced a light design on her flesh. He only intended to kiss her, to nibble gently and enjoy the husky tone that entered her voice as she tried to maintain the conversation with her sister. Through the phone he could hear Roxy arguing with her, telling Willow yet again that she shouldn't run away from her problems, that she needed to come home and fight back. Her sister told her she should go back to her former employer and go after the jerk who had gotten her fired, or at least come home so she knew Willow was safe.

His lips caressed Willow's skin, his hunger growing as her pulse fluttered gently beneath his lips. Willow's breathing had changed, quickening as she pressed back, closer to him.

"I have to go. I'll talk to you later." Willow hung up before her sister could say anything else. Tilting her head to the side, she gave him complete access to her neck. "God, I love it when you do that," she moaned. She squirmed slightly from her position between his legs.

Tell her now. Tell her the truth, how much you want her and how no one else has been able to satisfy you since you met her, his conscience screamed.

I will tell her. I'll tell her everything, he promised himself, lingering over the delicate pulse point. *But I just need one more taste. I'll die if I don't get one more taste of her and she runs away from me screaming.*

Despite his good intentions to tell her the truth, the temptation to taste her at least one more time proved to be too great to resist.

His teeth lengthened, sliding so easily into her neck that he had to force back a groan. As he suckled, drinking deeply, he had to silence the moans of ecstasy that threatened as her blood filled his mouth and he felt her arch back against him. Her ass started to rub against his hard cock as his suckling grew more insistent.

Silencing the voice inside his head that still continued yelling at him—promising him he only needed to confide in her and things would work out—he lost himself in her taste. Seth forced himself to close the wound before he got carried away. He was about to lick any remaining traces of blood from her neck when she surprised him by pulling away.

Pulling away from Seth, Willow was no longer lost in the pleasure of his lips on her flesh as something sharp slid across her neck. When she looked backed at him, her confusion increased.

His eyes were glazed, like he had just finished an entire bottle of wine in just a few minutes. She was about to question him about what he had done when she noticed a drop of something rolling down his chin. Putting her finger to his mouth, she wiped it away, growing anxious when she noticed it was red. Placing her fingers gingerly on her neck, in the spot that felt somehow scratched, she rubbed. Her eyes grew wide when she saw blood smeared across them.

She didn't wait for an explanation. Jumping off the couch, Willow practically ran across the room.

"You bit me! I'm not sure I want to be involved in something that kinky." Feeling slightly more comfortable now that there was a significant amount of space between them, she took a good look at him. Did his teeth appear longer, sharper than they had earlier? She allowed her hand to return to her neck. "What are you?" Her voice sounded higher than usual, even to her own ears as her hand remained protectively on the spot he'd just suckled.

"I can explain..."

"Explain what? You bit me! You—you bit me and I just wiped some of my blood off your mouth. Oh my God! What are you? Are you into blood games, because I don't remember any of this happening all week." She needed to calm down. She could feel herself becoming hysterical. She'd always thought that was more of an exaggeration, that people didn't still react that erratically in this day and age.

"Willow, please, calm down. I promise there is nothing to be afraid of. Please, come sit down and I promise we'll discuss this like mature adults."

"Like hell there isn't! There is no way I'm sitting back down beside you. I want some answers. Why did you bite me? Were—were you drinking my blood?"

One word was flashing across her mind.

Vampire.

Seth is a vampire. Or at least he thinks he is. It makes sense, part of her reasoned. "Oh my God. You're a...you're a vampire," she stuttered, her hand lowering from her neck. "But vampires aren't real." In her anxiety, she started wringing her hands. She looked down when she felt something sticky on them. Her fear grew as she saw traces of blood on both her hands thanks to her nervous habit. It looked like much more now that it was smeared over both of her hands. *Oh my God, this guy thinks he's a vampire!*

"I don't think I'm a vampire, Willow, I have always been one."

Willow almost swayed as Seth threw her own thoughts back at her. "It all makes sense now," she said, her voice low, as she spoke her thoughts aloud. She was talking to herself more than she was to him. "Why you never ate, why you said those things about vampires after that movie. Why you stay up all night, and sleep all day..." Her voice rose as her panic increased. "God, no wonder you were willing to do anything for me. What was I—an all-you-can-drink buffet?"

"Willow, sweetheart, it wasn't like that. I was going to tell you ..."

"When? When you had almost drained me? Or when you'd decided whether or not to change me? I can *not* believe I am having this conversation. I'd really like to wake up now, please." Closing her eyes she gave a humorless chuckle. "You know, if you'd asked me a week ago what I thought I would be standing in a room arguing with a guy about, I can pretty much guarantee that it wouldn't have ever included anything about a conversation about fictional creatures. Of all the things I thought I had to worry about with you, I never once even considered the possibility that you would kill me by draining my blood. I trusted you."

"Sweetheart, I'm not fiction. I am the figment of no one's imagination." He slowly stood and approached her.

Looking into her eyes, Seth reached his hand out toward her. "And if I wanted to drain you of your blood, I could have easily done so the first night you slept in my home. Sweetheart, please, just calm down."

"Don't do that. You don't get to do that anymore. You don't get to try to make me melt with your voice—or touch me anymore." She could feel her fear growing. "This wasn't the first time, was it? That you drank my blood, I mean."

He shook his head no.

"Tell me," she demanded, only barely resisting the urge to stomp her foot.

"I don't see how..."

"Tell me," she screamed.

"The first morning you were here I drank from you." He didn't look very happy with the confession.

"That's why I slept all day, isn't it?" Her panic increased as he nodded. "When else? When you 'kissed' my finger?" He nodded again. "Any other times?"

Seth shifted his gaze to her thigh. Her hand automatically followed his gaze.

"That's why I was so sore?" She lifted her hand to cover her eyes, but the sight of her blood had her quickly lowering it again. "This can't be happening to me. I'm a good person," she said to herself. "I—I have to go."

"Please, wait. I'll get a car for you."

"No! Stay away from me!" Willow ran to the elevator and continuously pushed the down arrow until the doors opened. "Just stay away from me." Inside the elevator she repeatedly hit the close doors button until the doors shut. She was terrified Seth would try to touch her again and she would simply melt into his arms. Even knowing what she did about him now, she could feel her body struggling. Unlike her mind, her body didn't know if it wanted to run back to him or start shivering with his betrayal.

Running out of the elevator as soon as the doors opened, she sped out of the lobby without paying attention to her surroundings or any stares she may be receiving. When she was safely outside she hailed a taxi, uncaring that she was only wearing Seth's shirt; that she didn't have shoes to protect her feet from the hard street or any money to pay for the ride. Giving the driver her address she pleaded with him to hurry, constantly looking over her shoulder to make sure Seth wasn't following her.

Her fear must have motivated the driver because in no time they were weaving through traffic in a manner that would have scared her if she weren't already afraid for her life. She didn't start to feel safe again until her building came into view.

"If you just wait right here, I'll get your money," she promised.

Exiting the cab with her, the driver stuck close to her side as she greeted the doorman, asking him to page her sister.

Ten minutes later Willow's sister was ushering her to the bathroom inside their apartment to clean her up.

"What the hell happened to you? Why is there blood smeared all over your neck and hands?" Roxy asked, her voice filled with concern.

Before Willow could stop her, Roxy put a washcloth under warm tap water and began to clean her neck.

"I see a rather dark mark on your neck," Roxy scolded her sister, "but no real wound. What happened? How the hell did you get blood on your neck? And where did you get the small scratch from? That couldn't possibly have been deep enough to leave any blood, much less enough to smear across your hands! Hell, it's already healing," she said leaning closer to Willow's neck. "I've seen deeper paper cuts." Roxy asked one question after the other, barely giving Willow time to answer.

Staring at her reflection in the mirror, Willow couldn't tear her gaze off the mark Seth had left. It was the only indication, other than the small scratch and the streaks of blood on the previously white cloth in her sister's hand, that she hadn't simply imagined the entire thing.

"I'm not... It's not mine," she stammered. She never had been able to lie well.

"Then whose blood *is* it?"

"That guy's. The one I was with. I guess I must have busted his lip when I was trying to get away from him earlier. While he was sucking on my neck," she added lamely. "His tooth must have grazed me when I pulled away."

"Well, good for you. But maybe you should go get tested just in case."

"Tested?"

"Yes. Does HIV ring a bell? I don't want anything happening to my little sis because of some jerk who didn't understand what stop means."

"Oh, yeah. Right. I'll go get a test done." For the second time that night panic set in. *Do vampires even get HIV or AIDS? Do they get any form of STD's?*

"Good. I'm glad you finally came back home. Of course, it would have been nice if you were wearing a little more than just a man's shirt... Poor Dennis down the hall is probably still picking up his jaw. When exactly did we switch roles? When did you become the wild one? Where are your clothes?"

"I left them. They just didn't seem important," she whispered.

"Would you like me to go with you to go get your stuff? Or maybe I can call Bruce, he used to play football. I'm sure he wouldn't mind playing bodyguard for an hour or so. You know he had that huge crush on you..."

"No. They aren't important." Looking at Roxy she added, "I'd rather not see him again."

"You're probably right. After all, clothes can be replaced." Roxy wrapped her arm around Willow's shoulders protectively. "I'm just glad you're back here safe. And if you ever need to talk, about what happened, or almost happened, I'll be here for you. As a matter of fact, I'll call Tanya and cancel for tonight," Roxy continued, ignoring her sister's protests.

"No," Willow said a bit more forcefully as her sister began to walk away. She tried to smile when she looked at her. "I'll be fine, Roxy, really. It's nothing a good night's sleep won't fix. Besides, I'd rather spend a little time alone, if you don't mind."

"Alright, but if you need me for any reason, any reason at all, I'll have my cell phone on all night."

"I'll be fine, sis. Go, have fun."

With one final look back at her, Roxy finally nodded and headed for the door.

When it was closed, and she was left alone in the apartment, Willow went into her room. As the reality of what happened hit her, she began to shiver. Lying down beneath the covers of her bed, she couldn't seem to get warm.

"It's just shock," she told herself. That's *all it is. After the scare you had tonight, is it any wonder your body is acting all strange?* Closing her eyes, she tried to get some rest, but couldn't get comfortable or warm.

Climbing out of bed, she went to the linen closet where they kept extra blankets. Willow added several extra blankets to her bed. Once she was mildly comfortable, and beginning to finally warm up, she drifted into a troubled sleep.

Chapter Seven

Willow was in a beautiful hallway dressed in nothing but a modest nightgown. Her lack of clothes didn't concern her as she looked around amazed until she saw the familiar figure in the distance. She didn't need to see his face to know who was waiting for her. She'd recognize him anywhere.

"Willow..."

"No. I don't want to be here..." Turning, she ran as fast as she could away from him.

But the path she took led her right back to Seth.

"Go away! Leave me alone!" she screamed.

"Willow I just want to apologize..."

She didn't want to hear the rest of his explanation. She tried again to run from him, from herself. Just the sight of him had her traitorous body screaming for his touch. She wanted to feel his hands sliding over her flesh, his mouth coaxing moans from her throat.

What does a little blood matter? What does it matter, when he can do such wonderful things to me? her body asked.

But every path seemed to lead back to him. When he appeared before her yet again, closer than before, she couldn't fight her body's need for him.

"Please, sweetheart, allow me to make it up to you..."

He sounded remorseful. Her body betrayed her. She went into his arms eagerly, unable to deny herself feeling them around her once again, comforting her.

As soon as his arms closed around her body, her senses roared to life, her pussy growing wet from the simple touch. Seth lowered his mouth to her ear and she moaned with pleasure.

"I am so sorry, sweetheart, can you ever forgive me for deceiving you?"

She couldn't talk, couldn't think as Seth kissed her, his teeth nibbling down her neck. She wasn't afraid that he would try to take another taste from her. After all, it wasn't as though he had caused her pain.

"Only a dream..." she moaned.

"This can be as real as you wish it to be."

She waited to feel his teeth slide into her flesh, but it never came.

"I'm not here for your blood." He chuckled. "But I will go crazy if I do not feel you beneath me." Seth tugged the modest nightgown off, not happy until it was on the floor in a heap beside her feet.

"You are so beautiful. Easily the most beautiful woman I have ever had the pleasure of knowing." He took her nipple into his mouth.

Arching her back, Willow tried to give his mouth easier access to her body, pressing closer to him unable to get enough of his touch.

His sharp teeth glided across the taut peak, his tongue quickly following the same path. The sensation caused her pussy to grow wetter, anticipating the feel of his tongue on her clit.

"What are you doing to me?"

"What would you like me to do to you?" He looked up from her nipple with a sly smile.

"I don't want you to stop," she admitted before she could control herself.

Seth picked her up and gently laid her down on a bed that mysteriously appeared behind them. He caressed every inch of her flesh with his hands, while Willow writhed beneath him. Again he lavished her breasts with attention before continuing down her body.

Her back arched high off the bed again when he nibbled on her navel. Covering her, Seth dipped his tongue into the crevice before he inched farther down her body. His talented hands and mouth had her moaning, squirming to get closer to him as her body screamed for him to thrust deep inside of her.

Thrashing her head from side to side, Willow could hear the needy moans that escaped her parted lips. Every place he touched, her blood turned into fire, and Willow was certain if he continued teasing her much longer, she would burst into flames.

Opening her eyes, Willow could feel sweat rolling down her face as her sister shook her. *No,* her body screamed. *Why did you have to wake me up now?*

"Willow. Willow, wake up."

"I'm up, I'm up. Why did you wake me?" She wasn't sure if she felt more grumpy or sorrowful that she had been woken from the erotic dream.

"You were practically screaming in your sleep. You looked like you were having a nightmare. Why do you have so many blankets on your bed?"

"I thought you were going out..."

"I forgot my ID. I'm going to call Tanya and tell her I can't go out tonight."

"Please don't, Roxy. I'm fine, really."

"I'll be back after I talk to Tanya." Ignoring her, Roxy left the room.

The reality of what she'd nearly done hit Willow hard. She had practically succumbed to his touch yet again. The man had turned her into an addict, craving his touch, his kisses as surely as some needed drugs. He was her "fix". Shaking her head, Willow firmed her resolve. No matter how much her body was still screaming for satisfaction, she refused to reenter her erotic fantasy with Seth. She climbed out of the bed and made her way carefully to the kitchen. Inside the small room, she began to make a pot of strong coffee.

CB80

"What is going on, Willow?" Roxy asked, her voice filled with concern.

"I don't know what you're talking about, nothing's wrong. Why would anything be wrong?"

"Don't play innocent with me. You haven't been sleeping well all week, the circles under your eyes tell me that. Pretty clearly, I might add." Roxy shot her sister her no-nonsense look. "Ever since you came back from that guy's place... What did he do to you?"

"Nothing." *He just fucked my brains out. Oh, yeah, and he drank my blood, but that's okay, because I got off while he was doing it. All of it. Even when he drank from me.* The coarse language didn't surprise her. She had been cursing like a sailor—inside her own mind—this last week as her bad mood increased. Ever since her sister had interrupted her dream. Like a true addict, she was going through withdrawals as she constantly fought her body's craving for Seth.

Though she didn't use coarse language in everyday speech, nothing would stop her from using the terms inside of her head. Sometimes Willow wondered if she even knew who she was anymore.

"That's just what I mean. I know you. I know you have more to say than just 'nothing'. We grew up together, remember? I was always the moody one, not you. Why won't you tell me?" Roxy looked hurt that Willow wouldn't confide in her.

Guilt washed over Willow, making her feel horrible for closing her sister out. Maybe she should tell Roxy what was going on.

Yeah, 'cause she'll believe you were bitten by a vampire, right? Another part of her brain scoffed. *What would you have done if she had told you the same thing just a month ago?*

The answer was simple. She would have rushed her sister to the nearest shrink, as quick as she could. Looking at the troubled expression on her sister's face, Willow decided to tell her part of the truth, to placate her. "Roxy, don't worry about me. I just need to work through a couple of things in my head. That's all. I'll be fine when I finally figure it all out. You really should go out. Don't let my funk keep you trapped in here instead of having fun."

"After what happened the last time? Uh-uh," Roxy shook her head vigorously.

A cold chill swept over her body. She just wasn't sure if it was from the memory of Seth's hands, or the fear of what she'd almost allowed to happen. Closing her eyes, she could still remember every detail of the dream clearly.

If she tried, she could still feel the things he'd done to her, feel his teeth grazing against her skin gently so he didn't hurt her. Forcing the memory away, she tried to forget what would have happened if Roxy hadn't woken her up when she did.

Since the dream, she'd refused to allow herself more than an hour or two of sleep at a time. She'd grown almost dependant on the pots of coffee she constantly kept full to help her remain awake. She was terrified that if she allowed herself to sleep he would be there. She wasn't sure if he'd be ready to pick up where they'd left off or if he would tease her body more until she was ready to release her grip on sanity for him.

But one of the things she feared the most was the unknown; not knowing exactly what "powers" he possessed. She knew he could read her thoughts, but could he knowingly enter her dreams? Was that dream the result of her subconscious trying to provide her comfort, or had he broken into her mind, forcing his way into her dreams? Her fear, combined with the massive amount of caffeine she drank daily now, kept her awake when her body was ready to fall over from exhaustion— even if she was only just barely functioning.

"Why don't you go out with us?" Roxy stared at her, breaking Willow out of her thoughts.

"What?"

"Where were you? Will, you need to get some sleep, you can't keep this up." Roxy's face was full of concern.

"I'm fine. You go on out, I'm not sure I feel like going out tonight." Sighing, Willow pressed forward. "Don't let me stop you from having fun. I can take of myself. And there haven't been any more...dreams, like the one you woke me from. I'll be fine," she insisted.

"Maybe I should take you to the doctor? Maybe that guy did something to you that you don't know about. He could have slipped some kind of wacky drug in your food. Maybe it's something that you haven't been tested for yet, and you're having some kind of adverse reaction to it. Willow, you haven't been the same since you met him. You're scaring me."

"Roxy..."

"Don't Roxy me," her sister yelled, losing her temper. "I've tried to support you. I've tried to get you to go out. I've tried everything I can think of since you came home. Nothing is working. Whatever happened, either talk about it or *let it go*. Move on with your life. It isn't as if you fell in love with him or anything." Roxy's mouth gaped open. "You didn't fall in love with him did you?"

"Of course not. That wouldn't be smart."

"No it wouldn't. Did you?"

Willow knew her sister wouldn't let the subject drop until she answered. "No, Roxy, I didn't. I barely know him."

"Willow..."

"Stop. I did *not* fall in love with him," she denied.

"It would explain your funk..."

"God, what will it take for you to stop?" she asked desperately, not willing to explore that particular line of questioning.

"Go out with us tonight. Get dressed and come have fun. Come see that the world hasn't stopped turning. Put a smile on your face." Roxy crossed her arms in front of her chest.

"Fine. I give. You win." Willow turned and sulked as she headed for her room. As she walked, she mumbled loud enough for her sister to hear her. "And they say the baby of the family is the spoiled brat... Clearly the people that started that rumor never met you."

Roxy's laughter followed her past the closed door. For a brief moment, Willow allowed herself to smile. It was good to hear her sister's laughter again, and if this was what it took for her to finally convince Roxy that she was fine, she'd do it.

Even if it was an outright lie and she was still far from being all right.

∞

Willow was finally beginning to relax. She hadn't been pleased when Roxy and Mary made her switch seats so she couldn't stare at the entrance, watching every man who entered The Grunge to make sure it wasn't Seth. At first she'd wanted to refuse, but they persisted until she moved. She'd been terrified he would walk in at any moment, but after an hour with no sign of him, she had finally lowered her guard.

Willow sipped on her soda as the other two girls flirted with men across the bar, smiling and winking at them over their drinks.

"Who's it going to be tonight?" Mary asked.

"Not me. I have to go in to work early tomorrow." Roxy sighed.

"Willow? Think you're up to it?"

"What? Oh, no. I am not playing that game again. Ever." She'd explained she would only play the once. But even if she hadn't already told them, she'd have refused. She would not risk potentially meeting another freak or weirdo again.

"Then it looks like it's you, Mary." Roxy smiled. "If you're determined to play tonight that is."

Smiling as she listened to the women arguing, Willow had to admit her sister had been right. Being out with the two of them had actually made her feel better.

The Night Crawlers were on the stage again, and their music added to her comfort. It wasn't their usual night to play. Maybe they'd simply decided to play on impulse, the crowd wasn't as big as the last time she'd seen them at the bar. But that wouldn't last much longer. The bar was quickly filling as word spread the band was having an impromptu concert.

No one was sure of where they came from, and Willow didn't care. She enjoyed their sound. The raspy voice of the lead singer helped to distract her from thoughts of Seth as it wrapped around her senses, lulling her, drawing her into the music and out of her depression.

Her feeling of content shattered as she felt a prickle on her neck. A shiver raced down her spine and somehow she knew Seth had just walked through the door behind her.

Seth couldn't believe his eyes. There she was, sitting with the same two women she'd been with the night they met. From the slight glimpse of her profile, he could see she was smiling as she began to nod in time with the music. Since the night she'd left him, Willow was never far from his thoughts. At first he wondered if maybe he was simply imagining her thanks to his all-consuming desire to see her again.

Standing perfectly still, blocking the entrance, he ignored the band as they played on the stage. He didn't care how many people they brought into his bar—or that he was preventing people from entering. He only cared about the one woman he couldn't take his eyes off of.

He'd tried to reenter her dreams after they were interrupted, but for some reason, he had been unable to find her again. He knew he could enter her mind, but refused to do that. Entering her dream was one thing. Dreams were just subconscious images that could be easily manipulated. Breaking into her mind, reading her thoughts to find out where she was or if she missed him as well, felt wrong. She should at least be able to feel safe in her own mind. And he had already betrayed her trust enough.

Still standing there, he wondered if he should approach her. What would her reaction be if he did? *She was so upset when she left...so distraught when she found out what I am... Maybe I should just leave her alone...*

As he watched Willow, her spine stiffened. The smile left her face and she acted as though someone had just thrown ice water on her, ruining her fun. It was as though she could feel him watching her. It made his decision for him. *I'll just leave her alone in peace. Willow has made it clear that she does not wish to be with me any longer. Now all I can do is hope she doesn't reveal my secret.*

His shoulders sagging, Seth walked over to the darkened corner where he typically sat and ordered a drink while waiting for Jason to arrive.

Unable to take comfort in the music, he gulped down the alcohol before the waitress could even set it on the table and ordered another to be brought to him.

He was on his second drink when he spotted Jason. As Seth watched, Jason approached Willow and squatted beside her. Instead of pushing Jason away, she spoke to him. Thanks to the Night Crawlers, there was too much noise for Seth to hear what they were saying.

Seth's teeth lengthened and the beast that had raged inside of him the last week roared to life. No man would touch his sweet Willow while he simply sat around and watched. His grip tightened on the table until he heard the first telltale creaks warning it was about to break.

No, his rational side tried to reason. *She left you. It isn't as if you can run over there, beat Jason until he's black-and-blue then throw her over your shoulder. You can't just stake your claim on her like you could've in the Middle Ages!*

Why not? the beast inside asked, its voice guttural. *Doesn't she at least owe me something? A chance to apologize, maybe a small sip from her? My hunger has not been sated since she left. Am I supposed to simply starve until I can no longer remember her taste?*

He sat there, battling with himself to gain control of the beast within. Finally, Jason stood and walked over to join him.

"I hope I haven't kept you waiting long," Jason said as he sat.

Instead of answering, Seth simply growled into his drink. He wasn't sure if it was directed to his friend or himself. His eyes narrowed as he caught a faint trace of Willow's scent coming from the other man.

"I can see you are in another good mood," Jason said sarcastically before ordering a soda from the waitress. "I didn't know the Night Crawlers were playing tonight..."

Seth grunted in response and tossed back the drink the woman had just placed in front of him in one long swallow. He didn't care what the band did. It didn't matter if there were a dozen people or more than a hundred in the room. He was only aware of one woman. But she refused to be near him.

As another song began, the too familiar ache spread through his stomach again. He'd been careful to drink before he entered the bar, but yet again the blood had not satisfied his thirst. No one tasted as sweet as Willow did. No one else had been able to ease his thirst, no matter how much he drank. He'd come damn close to draining the last few people from whom he'd drunk.

"Seth, you have got to get over this. Whatever happened between you and that girl is over, you need to stop..."

He wasn't sure how he looked, or why Jason had stopped speaking. He didn't care. Willow was walking toward him.

"May I join you?" she asked.

He couldn't help feeling a tingle of excitement. Would she sit on his lap again if he said yes? "Of course." His tingle froze as she sat on one of the unused chairs. Fighting back another wave of pain, Seth tried to smile. "Would you like something to drink?" He was amazed to hear his voice sound so calm, as the waitress brought Jason his soda.

"No, thanks. I won't be staying long."

Trying to appear relaxed, he leaned back in his chair, drinking in the sight of her. She looked as if she felt the same way he had since she left, as though she'd been living in the same hell. There were dark purple circles under her eyes even her make-up could not completely conceal. *Was that why I have been unable to find her? Has she been refusing to sleep?* For her to attempt such a feat proved how strong a will she had. It made him want to wrap his arms around her and protect and comfort her more than ever. He wanted to promise he would keep her safe and know that she believed him, that she trusted him.

Despite her apparent exhaustion, she was easily more beautiful than any other woman in the room.

"Um, I need to ask Seth a few questions..." She spoke hesitantly.

"I'll just go get a refill from the bar," Jason said, getting up from his chair and, taking his still full glass, walked across the room.

"What would you like to know?" Seth couldn't seem to keep the corners of his mouth from twitching upwards, into a small smile. This was similar to their first meeting. What else would mimic that first meeting? And by the old gods, she smelled delicious. His body couldn't help remembering her passionate response to his caresses and stirred to life. His teeth ached as he thought about her physical response to his bites.

"What did you do to me? Was that dream real?" she demanded.

"Yes, it was." Leaning forward, Seth decided he would be completely honest since he didn't know if he'd ever have a second chance. "I didn't mean to scare you. I simply wished to apologize for frightening you earlier. You did not stay long enough for me to do so in person," he explained.

"How could you find me like that?" Willow wore a bewildered expression, a look of concern slowly mixing in with it.

Seth shifted his gaze to her neck then back to her face in response.

Immediately she lifted her fingers to brush the spot where she had carried his mark. The move created havoc on his senses. Underneath the make-up, there was still a faint trace of it on her skin. Her eyes widened as she realized what he meant.

"So because of..." Her fingers brushed against her neck again as she hesitated. "You can enter my dreams anytime you want?"

"Yes," he told her truthfully.

"Damn." She swore under her breath. "Wow, I feel like I should move to Elm Street." He looked at her, eyes narrowing in confusion. "Like the movie," she explained slowly. "*A Nightmare on Elm Street*, Freddy Kruger..."

Shaking his head, he admitted he didn't understand the reference she was trying to make.

"Boy, you really don't watch much television. In the movie," she sighed, "there's a little rhyme. I won't go through all of it, but at the end it goes 'nine, ten, never sleep again'."

"I'm not sure I understand where you are going with this."

"The point is, I guess, I'll never be able to sleep again. I don't want to worry if there is going to be an uninvited guest inside my head, or my dreams." She leaned her head back, her eyes closing.

She stayed that way for several minutes, causing Seth to wonder if she had fallen asleep. Pleasure filled him at the thought of feeling her in his arms again as he carried her out of the bar, even if it was to simply put her in her friend's car.

"Sweetheart?" He called to her softly, not wanting to disturb her if she had fallen asleep.

"Don't call me that," she said, still not moving from her position. "Now back to the other question. What exactly did you do to me?"

"I'm not sure I understand what you mean."

"When you...drank, did you do anything else?" She opened her eyes and looked at him. She appeared so exhausted that his heart broke.

Cocking an eyebrow, he waited for her to explain. "You're not good for my ego. I'd have thought you'd remember exactly what else I did to you." He'd never forget her reactions—any of them. He'd dreamt of each minute detail every night since she left.

"I mean anything else." She blushed. "You know, something I didn't know you were doing." He was amazed at how much he missed seeing her blush. The gesture warmed his heart, until he thought about what she'd said.

Shaking his head, his voice was rough at her accusation. "I wouldn't do that. Not to you." He had to add the last part, even if she didn't believe him.

"Fine. Thank you for answering my questions. I guess I should get back to my friends now." Despite her words, she didn't move.

Seizing the opportunity, Seth tried to apologize again. "Willow, I am sorry that things ended the way they did..."

"Don't do this. I don't want to hear how sorry you are. I don't want to hear how you would change things if you could do them over again. I've heard the lines. And that's all they are. Just lip service to allow you to feel better about what happened. It's not as if..." Willow was interrupted by a loud growl from Seth's stomach. Unfortunately his stomach had chosen the precise moment that the Night Crawlers walked off the stage for a break to make its protest. Without the music blaring and people attempting to talk over each over, Seth knew it was too much to hope that Willow hadn't heard the embarrassing sound.

This time, it was his face heating up as it turned a dark shade of red.

"What was that?"

"Nothing," he said unconvincingly.

"Was that your stomach?" She looked at him skeptically.

"No," he lied again.

"Yes it was. Why would your stomach be growling? I thought vamp...I thought you preferred a *liquid* diet?"

"I do."

"Then why... Haven't you been eating?" He tried to ignore the concern in her voice, convinced he was simply imagining it.

"Is eating the right word?"

"Drinking or feeding would probably be more accurate," he replied automatically. His hands covered his stomach protectively, trying to prevent any more sounds from escaping.

"You haven't been drinking? Why?" she demanded.

"I have," Seth insisted. Trying to stand, his body wouldn't cooperate and he swayed dangerously. He gripped the edge of the table in an obvious attempt to prevent himself from falling.

"Where is that friend of yours when you *need* him? Or does he only come around when he can interrupt something?" Willow's anger emanated from her as she jumped from her seat and wrapped her arm around his waist to help steady him. She no longer seemed tired to the point of exhaustion.

He would have laughed if his stomach didn't feel so tight. She'd gone from being frightened of him, to concerned for him, to wanting to pummel Jason in just a few minutes. Willow looked adorable when she was furious. Especially when she was furious on his behalf. He wondered if she realized what she was doing but decided that at the moment it was enough just to feel her against his body. He wouldn't question the reason. Unfortunately her nearness intensified the hunger.

"Finally," she huffed as Seth saw Jason hurrying back over to the table.

"What's going on? What happened?" Jason sounded like he was about to start panicking. "What'd you do to him?" he demanded, glaring at Willow.

"No, really, I don't need any help steadying him. It isn't like he weighs a ton or anything..." she barked at Jason sarcastically as the man stood there staring at her instead of helping stabilize his friend. Thankfully he took the hint and went to Seth's other side.

"Let's take him to the back office."

Together they helped Seth get to the back of the bar, heading for the manager's office. As soon as the door was opened, and Willow saw the dust and cobwebs, she shook her head emphatically.

"No. How far is his place from here?" She directed the question to Jason as she struggled to help keep him straight.

"A few minutes, why?"

"We'll take him there."

"Really? Do you know how to drive a motorcycle? Can you drive one *and* balance him at the same time?"

"No, genius. I figured we'd take your car. You did drive here, didn't you?" The edge to her voice caused Jason to blush.

"Oh, right… I'm parked this way," he said as they shuffled Seth through a back door that led almost directly to the man's car.

"You would have a two-seater, wouldn't you? Jeez, compensating much?" She gave her best condescending look as she looked over at him, not trying to hide her glance to his crotch. "Let's see, our options are, you drive and I sit on Seth's lap, or I drive and you sit on his lap. But since I don't know where he lives I guess you *have* to drive."

They got him into the car and Jason walked over to the driver's side. "I thought you didn't want to be with him anymore," Jason commented as he fastened his seat belt while she was still trying to get herself situated inside the small car.

"Just because I don't want to be *with* him anymore doesn't mean I take any pleasure from his pain." She squirmed on his lap until Seth put his hand on her stomach, stopping her and pulling her back against him.

Chapter Eight

"Number one, I'm right here, I *can* hear every word you're saying. I'm weak, not deaf. Number two, sweet...Willow, if you keep moving, I will not be held responsible for what happens." Seth chuckled deeply as Willow instantly froze.

He was thankful they were able to get to his place so quickly. His cock was growing hard against her delectable ass, and he was sure she wouldn't appreciate that.

As soon as the car stopped, she opened the door and flew off his lap as though she were on fire. But no matter what her opinion of him was, she stepped closer to help him out of the car. Thankfully she moved backward, out of his way when Seth shook his head.

They were in the elevator when another growl came from his stomach and a cramp doubled him over, bringing him to his knees.

By the time the elevator doors opened, he was barely able to stand. Willow and Jason propped him up, helping him to slowly make his way through the apartment. He could smell the duo sweating by the time they reached the bedroom.

Seth collapsed onto the bed as though he were a rag doll, feeling as weak as a newborn babe. For the past few days his hunger had gotten worse. But this was the first time his stomach had ever growled like a human's.

Is this what humans feel when they are deprived of food?

In all of his life, he couldn't remember ever hearing of such a thing happening to a vampire. The stories said his people simply grew mindless, so wrapped up in their desire for blood that nothing else mattered until their thirst was sated. Those were the stories told to vampire children to keep them from starving themselves as humans did.

"What can we do for him? Does he keep any blood around here for emergencies?"

"I don't think so."

"Go check," Willow ordered as she began removing his shoes. When Jason was out of the room she spoke to him. "Don't get excited, I'm only taking off your shoes and socks. Nothing else."

Willow worked as she spoke. Feeling her hands on him, even in such a very non-erotic fashion, threatened his tenuous control. If not for all the pain he was in, he'd have pulled her beneath him that moment.

"There isn't any blood in the fridge," Jason said a moment later as he walked back into the room.

"Has he been drinking?"

"Yeah. I think he had three Scotches at the bar."

"Not drinking, *drinking*." With a sigh, she said, "Feeding."

"He said he has. But it's not like I'm actually there."

"Well, give me your wrist." Willow held her hand out.

"Why?" Jason looked at her warily.

"He needs to eat...drink...feed. Whatever. So give me your wrist." She held her hand a little closer to him.

"Why my wrist? Why not your wrist?" Jason's voice was higher than usual.

"Because *you're* his friend," she tried to reason, rolling her eyes.

"Well, he's already taken your blood before," he countered.

"Your friend is a vampire and you're telling me he's never taken a little...nibble?" She looked at him disbelievingly.

"Exactly. Ours is a business relationship. And he's like family. He's known all of my family. For generations. And never once has he drank from any of us."

"You know, you people have serious problems. Fine." Willow held her wrist up to Seth's mouth. "But this is absolutely the last time. I mean it."

When he didn't move to take her wrist Willow began to grow more concerned. "He won't take it. What, my blood isn't good enough now?"

"Both of you need to leave, now," Seth said. His voice was a bare whisper.

"Maybe we should listen to him," Jason told her. He inched away from his friend.

"Why? I'm not afraid. He's taken my blood before and never hurt me."

"Then why did you go running out of here dressed in just a shirt?" When she looked at him, Jason rolled his eyes. "Yeah, he told me about it."

Willow's face burned with embarrassment. "That's none of your business."

"Vampires don't react to hunger the same way we do," Jason told her, ignoring her outburst. "They tend to get mindless and uncaring of who they hurt until they get enough blood."

"Well, I'm not going anywhere. Do you happen to know, in your immense knowledge of vampires, how I can make him bite me?" Willow couldn't control the sarcasm in her voice. She was tired of the other man acting like an expert but refusing to be of any actual help.

Jason cleared his throat. "Stimulation is a...um...is a very good way," he stammered.

"Stimulation? Like what, rub his teeth? Oh... Wait, do you mean stimulation or *stimulation?*" Willow didn't think her face could become any redder. "Can't you just go to the kitchen and get me a knife? I can cut my wrist and stick it in his mouth. Wouldn't that work?"

"Probably. But I don't know if he'd be able to stop. I mean, if he's as hungry as I think he is. I've never actually heard him get so hungry that his stomach growled before."

"Great. Just great. *I* didn't want to go out tonight, but no, Roxy throws a tantrum and out I go. Then you have to come over to my table, where I was sitting quietly, not bothering anyone, and minding my own business. You just had to ask me to at least give vamp-boy a chance to explain. And like a fool I listen. Dammit, I stopped sleeping to avoid him. Now, here I am stuck with a vampire, that I broke all contact with, who will probably drain me dry, and my friends are probably wondering where I've disappeared to, again. And now, to top it off, I have to stimulate him. Could tonight get any weirder?" Willow was ranting as she began to pull her own shoes off. As she began to move over to unbutton Seth's jeans she looked at Jason, still standing in the room. Already furious, she didn't try to control her tone, a tiny piece of her glad to have an outlet to take her anger out on. "What, now you're going to watch?"

That seemed to have an effect because Jason turned around and walked out of the door, closing it tightly behind him.

"Okay, Toothy, you owe me big for this," she told him as she parted his jeans, uncaring of whether or not he heard her.

When his thick, beautiful cock came out, Willow's mouth watered. Her body seemed to scream to life. Lord, she had missed it—had missed him.

"Willow, you should go while you still can," Seth whispered.

"Not until you've eaten...drank, whatever," she told him before leaning down and licking a drop of precome from the tip. Taking him fully into her mouth, she watched him ball his hands into fists as he groaned.

Up and down, she caressed his cock, her tongue swirling around the tip as she lifted, almost removing it from her mouth. When his hips began to move with her, she took it as a good sign.

Sticking one wrist up near his mouth she was surprised when he didn't immediately bite her.

Increasing her movements, she rolled his balls with her free hand. Cupping them in her palm, she rubbed them when he was completely buried inside of her mouth. His hips flexed, meeting her mouth with more force. Sticking her finger into his mouth, she tried to feel around, attempting to find out if his teeth had become fangs yet.

She moaned around his cock as he sucked on her finger, his tongue stroking the digit.

Pulling her finger out of his mouth, she increased the speed of her mouth. She sucked on him harder, lost in the sheer pleasure of his response. Twisting her head, she tried to move from his touch as he fisted his hand in her hair, attempting to pull her off of him. She would not be denied. She'd wanted to feel him inside of her mouth since that first night. Growling, she continued to take him into her mouth until she felt his balls tighten.

She greedily swallowed every drop of cum that he released into her mouth, enjoying his taste. Giving one final, gentle suck on the head, her tongue flicked against the tip as she licked all lingering traces of liquid from his flesh. Resting her head on his thigh she lifted her wrist to his mouth once more. But still he didn't bite her.

"What's wrong now? I *know* you were stimulated."

Seth shook his head and chuckled slightly. "Wrong stimulation," he whispered weakly.

"So, what kind of stimulation do you need?" She sighed as she sat up. She didn't want to think about how much she had just enjoyed what she did. It was supposed to be a gesture of help, not for her own pleasure.

"You should go. Really, you don't have to do this," he told her, visibly fighting another cramp as he automatically began to cradle his stomach with his hands again. He curved his body as though trying to shift into the fetal position.

"I'm not leaving until you feel better. So you may as well just tell me." Moving to the side of the bed, closer to him, she stared down at his face.

Seth's mouth was set in a firm line. He obviously wasn't going to tell her. She got off the bed. Well, if he wasn't going to help her, she would just have to cheat...

Storming out of the room, she quickly found Jason. He was sipping one of the soda's Seth had bought for her as he lounged on the comfy sofa and watched television.

"Hey, I thought he didn't have a TV," she complained.

"Oh, he has them, but he doesn't watch them. Did you, ah... Is he..."

"Better? No. He said I gave the wrong stimulation," she sulked as she sat beside the man on the couch. "Let's be blunt, shall we? What exactly is the kind of stimulation that he needs?" Willow reached over and snatched the remote from Jason's hand and turned the television off.

"I was watching that," he whined. When her expression didn't change, he sighed. "Well, he needs to *want* to bite you..." Jason hedged.

"Okay... Can you be a little more specific?"

"What I mean is he needs—he needs to..."

"Are you always this articulate?" Her sarcasm grew with her annoyance. This man had walked in while she was naked but for a sheet and laying in Seth's bed—knew that she'd just performed some erotic deed with him—and still he acted modest around her.

"Are you always this much of a bitch?" he shot back.

"Actually, no. I've been told I have a very sweet disposition. But I can be rather nasty when I'm worried," she admitted grudgingly.

"What do you care if he gets better?" Jason turned on the couch to face her. "I'm not trying to be a dick, but the last I heard, you wanted nothing to do with Seth. And you said that what, twenty, maybe thirty minutes ago? All night, the entire time we've been trying to help him, you've just complained and made sarcastic remarks. You've made it clear you don't want to be near him, that he disgusts you, so why bother sticking around to help him?"

"Because, I want to help him," she admitted. "Look, I'm not sure how I feel about him being a vampire. And I sure as hell have more than a few problems with the fact that he didn't tell me *and* drank my blood without my permission. And even more questions about that. I don't know if I could ever date a vampire. But that doesn't mean I want to see him suffer either. I want to help him, Jason. I'll worry about the why's later."

"Fine. Look, I can't tell you what you need to do. I don't know exactly, since he's never drank from me. And, truthfully, I've never heard of him needing to be forced to feed. My best advice to you, just think of the times when he bit you before. Now that you know what he was doing, it should be easier for you to figure out what he needs to entice him." Jason took the remote back from Willow and cut the television back on, instantly channel-surfing once more.

Let's see... He bit me the morning he left a hickey, but I didn't really do anything. And I know he took a taste the night I bloodied my knuckle... But I put that wound there. And Jason already said he might not be able to stop himself if he's as hungry as we think he is. The last time we were making out... Should I go in and try to make out with him? No, he's in too much pain and it might take a while to get him to that point. I need something that will work almost instantly...

Willow looked down at her legs, praying for inspiration. When she looked at her thigh, it hit her and she wondered why she hadn't thought of it before.

Without a word to Jason, she stood and walked back to the closed bedroom door. Once inside, she stripped out of her jeans and climbed on the big bed. She left her thong on, hoping she would be able to present him with her thigh and that it would be enough. She sent up a silent prayer of thanks that she'd decided to wear underwear that night.

Funny, never thought I'd ever hope that a guy didn't want to eat me. Especially since that is exactly what he needs to do. She shook her head at the contradictory thoughts. *No, he doesn't need to eat me, he needs to drink from me,* she reminded herself, feeling much like she imagined a human sacrifice felt before they were placed on the altar.

Taking a deep breath for courage, Willow climbed on top of him and sat on his chest.

"What are you doing?" Seth asked without opening his eyes.

"Whatever I have to," she told him truthfully. "Now you can be a good boy and bite me, or I can make you bite me. Which will it be?"

"You can't make me bite you," he told her. She sat still, waiting for him to open his eyes. When he did, he lifted his head and looked at her, or more appropriately at her barely covered pussy. She could feel the moisture gathering between her legs from his stare.

Keeping her legs positioned just so, she made certain he had a tempting view of her, knowing her lace thong barely concealed anything from his vision.

Groaning, Seth closed his eyes as his head fell back to the pillow.

"What's it gonna be? Are we doing this the easy way, or the hard way?" She refused to allow him to block her out of his mind.

Instead of answering her, Seth turned his head to the side.

She decided to take the motion as a challenge. And she loved a good challenge.

Rising to her knees she repositioned herself at his shoulders. When he continued to stubbornly look away from her, she moved forward again. In this new position, when he looked at her—and she was sure he would look at her—his chin would brush against her clit.

She smiled when she saw his nose flare as he smelled her arousal. But still he refused to bite her.

A girl's gotta do what a girl's gotta do.

Closing her eyes, Willow remained on her knees, practically straddling his face. Reaching down, she clasped the hem of her shirt, slowly tugging it off, she allowed it to fall to the floor beside his bed. The bra quickly followed.

Well, here's another thing I never thought I'd ever do. Practically straddle a vampire's face, begging him to bite me, wearing nothing but a thong. But oh wait, the best is yet to come...

She smiled as an appropriate pun popped into her head.

"Alright, just so you know, since you refuse to cooperate, I'm taking matters into my own hands." Her hands behind her head, she released her hair from the tight ponytail she'd put it in and closed her eyes. Seth could watch, or not, but she would lose herself in a fantasy. *The better to tease you with, my dear...*

She tilted her head back until she knew the silky strands of her hair would be tickling his chest. Then she slowly brushed her fingertips down her neck and chest to her breasts. Eyes still closed, Willow circled her nipples with her nails then tugged on them lightly. In her mind—her fantasy—it was Seth's hands teasing her body.

She couldn't stop the low moan as her nipples tightened deliciously. Tugging on the tight buds the same way he had when he teased her, a jolt of pleasure zoomed straight down her body to her open pussy. She almost whimpered when she felt Seth's chin brush intimately against her as he finally turned to watch.

Releasing one nipple, Willow brought her hand up to her face. She used a single finger to stroke her mouth, tracing her bottom lip before she sucked it into her mouth. Willow made certain to get her finger nice and wet, before lowering it to her nipple once again. The combination of the moisture from her finger and the cool air against the taunt bud had her once again moaning. With a slight smile on her face, she repeated the gesture with the other side.

She knew Seth was becoming more involved in watching her when he reached up, caressing her hips and ass. She decided to allow him the small gesture, but nothing more. *He had, after all, chosen to do things the hard way. And,* she smiled a wicked smile, *I did give him every opportunity to cooperate.*

She continued to tease her breasts for another minute or so, then slowly trailed her fingers down, under her breasts and over her stomach, working her way ever lower. At her navel, she stopped to circle it, teasing it as he had seen her tease her clit. Beneath her, Seth's breathing grew harsher, slightly more rapid, giving her the confidence to continue.

A sound of pleasure came from deep in her throat and she made no move to silence it. She smiled as she remembered him telling her how much her moans aroused him.

Willow allowed her nails to skip over her skin, following the curve of her underwear, across her thighs and back up. She enjoyed the feeling of them scratching her skin lightly.

Seth used his hands in an attempt to bring her closer to his face.

"Uh-uh," she purred, her voice husky. Opening her eyes, Willow looked deeply into his. "You don't get to play until you eat."

His hands froze.

He wants to try to play hardball, does he? Well, I'll fix that. At least he didn't release me completely, so I must be getting to him. Time to take this game a little further.

Pulling her underwear to the side, she made sure he had an unimpeded view of what she was doing. Sliding her finger across her wet slit, she never took her gaze from his face as he watched her finger hungrily. Parting her nether lips, she teased her clit, her smile growing larger as he began kneading her ass. She brought herself close to orgasm, growing wetter because she knew he was watching every movement of her fingers.

Bringing the finger she used to tease her clit to her face, she smelled it, moaning. Waving it under his nose, she was rewarded with a growl.

"You know, I don't know about anyone else, but I really like the way I smell." She brought her finger up to sniff it, once more lowering it to tease her body.

This time as she began to circle and tug her clit, her hips moved in time with her fingers.

Once again Seth tried to pull her closer to his mouth, lifting his head slightly as well.

"Tsk, tsk, what a bad boy. You know the rules, show me your teeth. Let me feel them against my skin," she coaxed.

Again he fell backward, still trying to refuse his hunger.

Well she wouldn't let him. It was time to play dirty.

Leaning down, Willow slipped her finger deep inside her soaking wet pussy. Just feeling his breath against her sensitive flesh after denying herself twice had her poised and ready to come. She swirled her finger deep inside, making sure to get it nice and juicy. Pulling it out, she waved it under his nose.

"Is this what you want? Do you want to taste me on your lips, on your tongue? Maybe the reason you can still resist my temptations is because you've forgotten what I taste like?" Sliding the digit over his lips, she smiled as his tongue darted out for the slight taste she had left him. His eyes grew dark, filling with passion and raw hunger.

Pushing her finger back inside her dripping pussy, she determined to tease him again. This time she slipped the digit between his lips, moaning deeply as he sucked the juices from it, his sharp teeth grazing her skin. Deciding her finger was clean enough, she pulled it back out of his mouth, ready to tease him with another small taste. After she played a little longer, that is.

But Seth had different plans. Faster than she could have believed possible given his earlier weakness, he lifted her, threw her on her back on the bed, and put his head between her legs. Before she could utter a syllable, he'd ripped her underwear from her body and threw the ragged pieces of lace across the room.

He lowered his head to her pussy. Clamping her thighs together tightly, Willow allowed her hands to grab fistfuls of his hair, stopping him. She refused to give in, no matter how badly she wanted to. This was a game she *would* win.

"You know the rules."

Growling deep in his throat, he glared at her. Ordinarily the sound would have scared her. But right here, right now—with him—it only made her wetter. His nostrils flared, as though he could smell the increase in her arousal.

Parting his lips, he opened his mouth and showed her his long, beautiful, sharp teeth. Loosening her grip, she wove her fingers through his hair, guiding him to the sensitive spot where her leg met her torso. It was the same spot he'd marked her before.

She screamed in pleasure from the fierce orgasm that racked her body as his teeth pierced her flesh.

Seth drank greedily from her, and she could not keep her body still. The sensations were intense, so erotic that she felt another orgasm building with lightning speed. Then his fingers were there, plunging deep within her as he continued to drink from her.

Crying out his name as wave after wave of intense pleasure raged through her, she was still riding them when his tongue slid over her skin. Shifting his head, he teased her incredibly sensitive clit with his tongue.

He removed his fingers only long enough to slide his tongue deep inside her. His razor-sharp teeth grazed against her flesh and his tongue followed.

He didn't stop his teasing until her body shook with her fourth orgasm.

Crawling up her body, he captured her mouth with his, tongue thrusting inside aggressively. The taste of herself on him—both her cream and her blood—drove her crazy. When he thrust his cock hard and deep into her, she cried out, the sound swallowed hungrily by him.

This was no gentle, sweet loving meant to bring them both to orgasm slowly. This was hard and fast, full of the rough pleasures they both needed at the moment.

As Seth pounded into her body ruthlessly, Willow met his hips with as much force as she could.

Growling into her mouth, Seth increased the pace of his thrusts. After a few minutes, she felt him explode within her.

They lay on the bed, panting and covered in sweat, Seth's hard body pressing her softer one down into the mattress.

For the first time since she'd found out the truth about him, Willow finally felt safe again. Unable to fight her body any longer, she was asleep before he withdrew from her and rolled them over.

Chapter Nine

"Mmmm," Willow moaned as she snuggled back into the chest behind her. *Life is good,* she thought sleepily. She felt safe and warm. She felt...whole. Happily she drifted back to sleep.

A knock on the door stirred her again a little while later.

"Go away, Roxy, I don't want to wake up. I'm having the most delicious dream," she called out sleepily, pulling the covers higher on her body, almost covering her head.

She heard the door crack open then a very masculine chuckle. "Well, my name isn't Roxy, and from the looks of this room, it wasn't a dream."

Opening one eye, she recognized Jason approaching the bed. She began to sit up but froze as she saw her ruined underwear hanging from his finger.

"I take it you were able to entice him to cooperate?"

Keeping the covers pressed tightly against her naked body, she sat up and looked around. Seth was nowhere to be seen. What was going on?

Her memory came rushing back. Seth had been sick. He'd needed to drink, and she'd had to entice him into drinking from her. Then they had had the most incredible sex of her life. And that was saying a lot, considering their previous encounters—before she'd run practically screaming from him.

"Will you just leave so I can get dressed?" Jason stepped closer, picking up her bra, chuckling when she snatched it from him. Turning, he began to leave but she stopped him. "Wait. Where's Seth? What time is it? Is he feeling better?"

"Make up your mind," Jason teased, looking back at her. "Either you want me to stay or you want me to leave." When she scowled at him, he chuckled again. "I'll answer all your questions, after you get dressed." Taking a deep breath, he amended, "Make that after you shower and get dressed." He laughed and closed the door, narrowly avoiding the pillow she threw at him.

Twenty minutes later, Willow walked out of the bedroom, feeling sore, but rested.

"Oh, good, food," she said right before she began to attack the food Jason had arranged on the dining room table. "Tell me what's going on, Jason," she said between bites and after a sip of soda.

"It's about midnight." Willow looked at him in confusion. "You and Seth have slept all night and day. He got up and left no more than an hour and a half ago." Shrugging, Jason continued. "He looked better, but refused to tell me where he was going."

"I need to use the phone," she stated as soon as her hunger was eased. Standing, Willow shook her head before walking away from the table. She paused at the door. "Is there any chocolate in this place? I don't know why, but I'm having a serious chocolate craving."

"It could have something to do with how much blood Seth took. I'll see if I can find you some while you call whoever you need to. And if there isn't any here, I'll call Seth's cell and tell him to pick some up."

"Thanks." She smiled, appreciating the offer. She wasn't sure she was up to talking with Seth just yet, and not over the phone. That just seemed too impersonal. Especially after what they'd experienced the night before.

She went into the comfy room and curled up on the couch. Willow really didn't want to call her sister, but she knew if she didn't Roxy would worry. And she couldn't have that on her conscience.

"Hi Roxy, it's Willow," she said as soon as the phone stopped ringing.

"Where the hell are you? Are you alright? What did that guy do to you? Tell me how to get there and I'll come pick you up. I have five former football players ready to back me up at a moment's notice."

"Calm down. Remember I told you I needed to work through some things? Well, that's what I'm doing. Please don't worry about me, Roxy."

"Don't worry? Don't worry, she says! First you disappear for a week, then you barely sleep for another week. Then—then you just disappear with the guy you stayed with. The one that messed you up in the first place, and you tell me not to worry? Willow, I demand that you tell me what's going on this minute," Roxy said in her best big-sister voice.

"Roxy, calm down."

"Don't tell me to calm down. This isn't like you, Willow. I'm the one who just runs off with a guy without telling you where I'm going or how long I'll be gone. I don't understand how you were always so calm about it all the time. I'm going crazy not knowing what's going on." The worry in Roxy's voice tore at her.

After a deep breath, she answered. "I was able to stay calm because I trusted you. I knew if you needed help you would call me. And that I would be right there for you the minute you did. I knew that you had to live your own life, make your own mistakes. Let me do that now. Please, trust that if I need you I won't hesitate to call," she pleaded.

"I do trust you, Willow." There were tears in her sister's voice. "But what if you can't get to a phone when you need me?"

"That's a chance I have to take. It's one you'll have to let me take. I'm not a little girl anymore. And I need to work through this my own way."

"Alright. Just please come back safe and happy. Or at least, not depressed anymore." After a moment, Roxy sighed. "Hell, I don't care. Just come back."

"I'll talk to you soon, Roxy."

"Will?"

"Yes?"

"When did you become the big sister?"

Giving a small chuckle, Willow sighed. "I wouldn't go that far. I've learned a lot from you. And there's nothing wrong with the big sister being the wild one. You never were very conventional."

She said goodbye and hung up the phone, laying back against the couch and closing her eyes. *Did I do the right thing? Should I just disappear into the night now that I know—well, think—Seth is going to be all right? Do I even want answers to some of my questions?*

Feeling around, she found the remote tucked into the side of the couch and turned the channel to an old movie she'd seen many times before. As she watched, she tried to fight back a yawn, unsuccessfully.

Why did I care so much about him being sick? Just what exactly do I feel for him?

Before she could answer any of her own questions, Willow was sleeping once again.

ℭ℘

Riding on his motorcycle, Seth dreaded calling his mother. He hated having to call her with such an awkward question, but he didn't know whom else he could ask. With a reluctant sigh, he pulled the motorcycle over and took the cell phone out of his pocket. Bringing the number up on speed dial, he refused to give himself a chance to second-guess his decision.

"Hi, Mom," he began.

"Seth Baker, or Brown, or whatever you're calling yourself these days, do you know how long it's been since you called me?" His mother's voice scolding him over the phone caused him to cringe.

"It's been—"

She cut him off. "It's been over thirty years, young man. Do you know how worried I've been about you? You would think that my youngest son would call at least once a decade. But no. Mr. I'm-almost-eight-hundred doesn't think his poor mother still worries about him. Your brother Angelo checks in with me now and then." She sniffed, "Even Thomas comes by for dinner every few years. But not you. No, my baby, the youngest of all my children is far too old for anything like that. Do you know how worried I was? I was getting ready to send your brother Raphael to track you down. Who knows what could have happened to you. If you don't check in with me more often, young man, I will track you down myself and then may the gods help you. You aren't too old for me to put over my knee, you know."

Throughout his mother's lecture Seth couldn't help but feel horrible that he hadn't called his mother earlier. He honestly hadn't believed she would be this worried about him.

"...could have been caught in the sunlight, or by one of those strange humans who are determined to stake us. Why did your cousin Vlad have to brag so much? If it weren't for him there would never have been a book, and

151

no vampire movies... His mother still cringes whenever someone brings that up, the poor dear. Well, it doesn't set everything right, but I heard he's still locked in his bedroom, and she only sends up old men every few days to feed him. None of the pretty young things that he used to drink from, I can guarantee you that. Teach him to blab our secrets to everyone... Oh, and your sister Grace sent me the most delightful pictures of her children—"

"Mom, I wanted to ask you something. It's kind of important," Seth interrupted her gossip. Now that her lecture was over, his mom was once again her usual bubbly self. And he needed to ask his question before the conversation turned into her asking when he was going to have children of his own.

"Of course, baby, what did you need to know?"

"I was wondering if you would tell me that old bedtime story I used to love."

His mother chuckled. "Almost eight hundred and you still want to hear that old legend?"

"I tried to remember it, but I couldn't." He paused. "It's really important, Mom. Please?"

"You always did say that." She laughed. "Alright." She sighed as only a mother can. Clearing her throat, she began her story. "Many years ago, so long ago that not even their names are remembered, long before my great-grandmother's time, there was a powerful wizard. He fell in love with a beautiful maiden, with hair the color of the sun and eyes the color of the sky on a clear summer day. For a while the wizard watched her from afar, marveling that he was only able to see her dancing under the moon. Not once did he ever see her during the daylight, no matter how hard he tried. He'd started to wonder if she were some kind of dream. But after a while, he finally gathered his courage and approached the maid. Instead of being afraid when he approached her, she laughed with him. They spoke until the first rays of dawn appeared in the sky. When he asked if he could see her again, she promised she would return the following night.

"Weeks passed and always, the wizard was waiting in the meadow when she arrived. They were often seen dancing under the light of the moon. It didn't take long for both to begin looking forward to their time together beneath the night sky, of being kissed by the moonlight.

"You must remember, this was long before things such as witchcraft and dancing were seen as sinful, as evil. Every night they fell more deeply in love. Finally, one night after the wizard swore his undying love for her, the maiden decided to tell him her most protected secret. She told him about her hunger for blood, how she would never be able to see the sunlight because it would kill her.

"At first the wizard scoffed at her. Thinking the maiden was simply trying to scare him, he took several steps away from her, trying to decide what he should do. He'd heard of such creatures before, but they were always monsters. Vicious beings who wouldn't hesitate to kill because their lust for blood was all-consuming. How could this beautiful, gentle maid be such a creature, he wondered. Turning to her, he asked for proof of what she said. Before he had time to blink his eyes, the maiden was once more beside him, pulling his head down to her own for a kiss. In the kiss, she allowed her hunger for him to show; she allowed her teeth to lengthen. The wizard gasped, pulling away from her as he tasted the coppery blood in his mouth from where her razor-sharp teeth had scratched his lip.

"She walked closer to him, stepping back into his embrace. The wizard tried to protest when she kissed him again, tried to warn her of the blood in his mouth. His eyes grew wide as he felt her tongue glide across the cut, just before she pulled away. The wizard could barely believe what was happening as he realized the cut was gone.

"He asked her from where she usually fed. 'The neck', she replied, praying that her love wouldn't find her repulsive. 'Will it hurt?' he asked. 'I cannot allow you to make such a sacrifice for me,' she cried. The wizard walked to her, tilting her head up. 'I swore my undying love for you. I would give you the Moon Goddess herself if I could. It will not harm me to allow you to take a bit of my blood.' The maiden was moved to tears, which her wizard gently dried with his handkerchief.

"With as much gentleness as she could, the maiden placed her mouth over the strong pulse in his neck. As her teeth slid into his flesh, the maiden and the wizard felt a bond form between them. One so strong it felt as if the very gods themselves could not break it. She pushed her thoughts out, directing them toward her love, images of them kissing, of slipping her dress off and allowing him to see her body naked in the moonlight. After taking only a few sips, just enough to ease the hunger caused by the blood from his lip, she closed his wound and looked at him anxiously.

She asked in a soft voice, 'Did it hurt?' 'No, my love,' the wizard assured her. The couple continued to meet every night, but the maiden refused to drink from her love again, afraid that she would do him harm if she drank from him too frequently. Though he understood her fear, he didn't want to think of her starving herself for his sake. He asked only one thing of her, that she only drink from other women. Holding her in his arms, he told her he couldn't bear to think of another man feeling such pleasure with her. One night, just over a week after her first taste of him, the wizard noticed his maiden was terribly weak. As he remembered their previous trysts, he recalled that each night she seemed to grow weaker, despite her assurances that she was feeding regularly.

"Then the strangest thing known to vampires happened. For the first time in remembered history, her stomach growled. The wizard was nearly frantic with fear. He called a strong soldier over to her, fearing that the oath he had made her swear was what weakened her. He wondered if women's blood was too feeble for her. If her pain was a result of his jealousy. If it were, he swore he would never forgive himself for such selfishness, for risking her life because of his possessiveness.

"With help from the wizard, and a lingering kiss, her teeth lengthened and she drank from the soldier, careful to close the wound and erase any memory of the event. When the soldier left, confused and wondering why he had left his post, the wizard held her close to him. When his arms loosened around her waist, she collapsed to the soft grass. She'd become so weak that she could not even stand on her own.

"He knew his love had drunk from the soldier, he had seen it with his own eyes, but it didn't seem to help. In despair he called to the Moon Goddess, pleading for the answer to the cure for his love.

"In a blinding flash, the goddess appeared, in a flowing gown the color of moonbeams. She had heard his plea, and looked deep into his heart. 'Do you truly love this daughter of the night?' the goddess asked him. 'I do, my goddess.' 'The only thing that can help her is blood. Her hunger is strong, almost unbearable, and soon she will be lost to it. She will go crazy with her need, but none will satisfy her thirst.'

"The wizard looked up at his goddess, unashamed as tears spilled from his eyes. 'I would gladly trade my life for hers, Goddess.' 'You need not die for your love. You must live for her. It is only your blood that will ease her hunger.' 'I do not understand,' the wizard told her.

"The goddess smiled with infinite patience. 'There is a bond between you. It is rare for her kind to find their perfect match, their perfect mate. When she drank from you, a bond was forged, so strong, that it has erased all need for the blood of any other. You are Blood Mated to this young vampire, wizard. Only your blood will ease her hunger.'

"The maiden had listened quietly as her goddess spoke, her eyes growing wide as her goddess told the wizard how to cure her. In a weak voice, the maiden asked 'But what if I drink too much?' 'You'll know when to stop,' the goddess reassured her. 'Your love for him will assure that.'

"True to the Moon Goddess's word, as soon as the maiden drank from her love she felt stronger. For months the couple lived in peace, binding their lives together under the light of the full moon, knowing that the goddess was looking down on them, smiling and blessing their union. The goddess even blessed them with a babe, the ultimate symbol of their love.

"But their happiness was not to last. Three years later, not long after the birth of their daughter, a stranger and his son came to their house. When there was no answer to his knocking, he walked inside, catching the maiden while she drank from her husband. In a rage, the man called her an unnatural beast and drove his sword deep into her body. So deep that it became buried in the wizard as well. Before her eyes, she had to watch her husband, her Blood Mate, her only true love die. Her rage grew so fierce that her eyes were said to have turned blood red.

"Pulling herself off the blade, in a frenzy she ripped open the man's throat, uncaring that his blood would do her no good. Letting him fall lifelessly to the floor, her grief began to consume her until she noticed the child cowering in a corner. His father's blood was splattered across him.

"At once she tried to pull him into her arms, to comfort him. But he would not go. Instead he backed away from her as much as he could. Sensing he was not yet ready to hear her story, instead she went to comfort the babe that lay near her bed. Days passed, and finally, after several nights of the widow feeding him and being kind to him, showing the boy that she meant the child no harm, he grew braver. He saw how gentle she was with the small baby, and eventually the boy finally grew courageous enough to ask her why she had killed his father.

"With tears in her eyes and voice, she told the boy her story, rocking her child the entire time. The boy watched as the widow bit her finger and allowed the babe to drink her blood. She told him all about her love and the Moon Goddess's words. She explained all she could about her people, stories that she had only ever spoken of with her wizard. She explained how his father had condemned her to a slow death of starvation when he killed her husband, her Blood Mate.

"As she finished her tale, leaving out no detail of her life and her people, no matter how small, the widow handed the boy a box. She told him that she wanted him to have all that belonged to her and her wizard.

"The boy cried at her heartbreaking tale, and tried to stop her as she opened the door. The first rays of light were already turning the sky pink. 'Don't. You'll die,' the boy pleaded, having forgiven her for killing his father now that he understood why she'd done it. 'I was condemned to death the moment my love died. I would rather see the sunrise once in my life than risk another innocent life because of my hunger.' She caressed his face. 'Even now I feel the hunger trying to control me, whispering in my ear to ease this horrible thirst.' Giving him a motherly kiss on the cheek, she placed her child gently in his arms. 'I have only one request,' she told him. 'Please watch over my child. I do not know if you will ever meet another of my kind, and I cannot bear the thought of her life being ended so soon. She is all that I have left of my sweet wizard.' A single tear of blood rolled down her cheek.

"The boy swore to protect the child with his life. After telling him how to care for her precious daughter, and giving them both one final kiss, she stepped outside. He wanted to run to her, wanted to be with her so she would not die alone, but he knew he could not take the babe into the sunlight or he would condemn her as well. Tears flowed freely down his cheeks as he watched the widow burn in the rising sun, while he stood safely in the shadows of her home.

"True to his word, the boy took great care of the baby girl that had been entrusted to him, calling her his sister whenever someone asked about her. He told her the story of her mother and father, of their love, every morning before she fell asleep. The years passed, and he aged, but the girl remained young. He was careful to never stay in one place too long, terrified of someone finding out their secret and taking away the only family he had. Throughout his life he did everything he could to give her anything she wanted.

"When she was old enough, he held her in his arms as he retold her the story of her people. Everything the widow mentioned about her people, her parents and how she came to be in his care. As time went on, and the girl grew into a beautiful woman, he began to claim her as his daughter, then, finally his granddaughter.

"All too quickly it became time for her to make her own promise. As the boy, now an old man, lay dying he made her swear to tell the story of her mother and father to her own children—should she have any. And to any of her people that she should encounter. He made her promise not to let their story, their love be forgotten.

"The girl kept her word to the man who had always loved and protected her. She knew he wasn't her father, but she'd loved him as such for her entire life. She knew in her heart that her true father would not mind. Eventually she met another of her kind and fell in love with him. She passed the story on to her love, then her own children, always careful to include the love she felt from the boy. She explained how he'd cared for her, how much she loved him and how he was the only father she had ever known. Through the generations, the sacred story has been passed down from mother to child, reminding us that love is a precious gift from the Moon Goddess. And that though we may feel anger, though we may be tempted to lose all control and give our rage freedom, we must be careful to never hurt an innocent. Because they do not deserve our punishments."

Seth sat on his motorcycle in tears. The story he had loved so much as a child had new meaning now. The part of him that had always scoffed at such a love, such a perfect mate being out there was silent. His heart broke for the nameless maiden and her wizard—and their fate. He knew exactly how the wizard felt when he thought he was losing his one true love. How the maiden must have felt, when he was taken from her.

Wiping away his tears, he wondered if he would ever be as brave as she was.

"Why did you want to hear that story?" his mother asked, her voice once again normal. "I thought you had grown too old for such a fairy tale centuries ago."

"I was wrong," he said, choking back the emotion in his voice.

"Seth, baby, what's wrong?" He could hear the worry in her voice.

"Nothing, Mom." He tried to keep his voice emotionless. There was nothing his mother could do to help, now that he knew he was "Blood Mated" just like the maiden and the wizard. He didn't want her to worry needlessly.

"You never were a good liar, at least not to me. You're a grown man. I understand if you don't want to tell your old mother. But promise me you'll call me again soon. After whatever's bothering you has been taken care of."

"Yes, ma'am. I love you, Mom."

"I love you too, baby. Come home for a visit soon. You can tell me all about what's going on then."

His mother hung up without waiting for a response. He was thankful he wouldn't have to lie to her again. He was afraid he wouldn't be able to keep the promise to visit her, and thankful he'd at least had one final chance to tell her he loved her.

No sooner had he hung up the phone than it rang again.

Looking at the caller ID in confusion, he saw his own phone number.

"Hello?" Could Willow be up and trying to call him? Dare he hope that she wanted to stick around to talk to him?

"Hey man, how are you doing?"

"What do you need, Jason?" Seth still felt too raw to hold a casual conversation.

"You need to make a stop. This lady of yours is feeling a rather large craving for some chocolate."

Seth promised he would stop and hung up the phone.

A couple hours later Seth walked into his apartment, arms loaded with chocolate and movies. When Jason mentioned that his Willow had a severe craving for chocolate, he had stopped by the next store and practically bought out the entire stock in the candy aisle. He wasn't sure what she liked and hadn't wanted to buy the wrong thing by mistake. On impulse he also stopped by an all-night video store and rented *Nightmare on Elm Street*, parts one and two. He was surprised to see just how many sequels the movie had, and hoped that those two would help him to understand the reference Willow made earlier.

As he walked by, he noticed her curled up on the couch, the credits to some movie rolling across the screen.

Quietly, he took the chocolate and movies into the kitchen.

"Oh great, you remembered to pick up some chocolate. Do you think you bought enough?" Jason teased. "Wow, you got the good stuff." Jason reached for a dark chocolate and raspberry candy bar. He shot Seth a dirty look when his hand was smacked away.

"You don't get any."

"Wow, you have it bad. Now, do you want to tell me what's going on? Why were you...whatever you were, earlier? And why did you just leave as though someone were trying to kill you?"

"It's a long story." Seth sighed.

"You're in luck, I have all night." Jason leaned on the counter and eyed the heap of chocolate, but didn't reach for any.

"Well I don't. I need you to take Willow back home."

"Why?"

"Just do it, Jason," he said irritably.

"Nope, not until you tell me why. She deserves to know too. She took a big chance with you. She risked her life for you. She was really worried, Seth, and you just left without saying a word."

"She shouldn't worry about me. And you shouldn't come by for a while. It's going to be rough around here."

"Well aren't you Mr. Cryptic," Jason huffed.

"You have been hanging around Willow entirely too much." Seth had to fight the surge of jealousy he felt at the thought of his Willow being with some other man.

"Wow, you rented movies, too. What did you get?" Before Seth could stop him, Jason grabbed the DVDs and frowned. "You got *Nightmare on Elm Street?* Only you could go into a video store and get a movie that has been around forever. Why didn't you get something newer?"

"I want to see this one," Seth told him simply, taking the movie from his hand.

"And just what made you have this sudden burning desire to watch *this* movie? You always refused to let me watch it when it was on cable. You said something about television and movies being nothing but a waste of time and told me to go read a book." Jason sulked. "Do you know how many times I've had to listen to you talk about the days when there was no television? How people were excited if they learned how to read, or could find a book—any book—to read? More times than any man should have to, I'll tell you that. Damn. Did my history teachers love it when I had to spend time with you."

"That was different. You were a child and your parents trusted me to keep you safe. And I wish to watch it now."

"Why?" Jason wouldn't seem to let the subject drop, he seemed determined to get an answer.

"I want to hear a rhyme. Does it matter?"

"Wow, you woke up on the wrong side of the bed. You'd think after waking up with a beautiful woman naked and lying across you, your temper would improve," Jason grumbled. "But no, you have to go and act worse than you did when she avoided you."

"That was different." Just how many times would he be allowed to get away with using that phrase in this conversation? "And how did you know she was lying across me?"

"I looked in on you two—just to make sure you were both in one piece. How is it different now?" Jason returned to the previous subject.

"It just is. Look, just take her home. I'll call you when it's safe to come around me again." His heart broke as he lied to his friend, knowing it was perhaps the last time he would ever see him.

"Fine. I'll go. But there are two things I won't be doing." He grabbed the jacket he'd kept in Seth's closet for emergencies and began to put it on. "First, I won't be waiting by the phone for your call." Jason walked over to the elevator. "And second, I won't be taking her anywhere. You want her gone, you tell her. She damn well deserves to hear this from you after what happened last night. To quote what you always tell me, 'It's your mess. You clean it up'."

Climbing into the elevator, Jason shook his head as the doors closed.

Seth was left standing in the middle of the hall.

Now what am I supposed to do? He was tired after his ordeal the night before. Who knew feeling human sickness could be so tiring?

Looking over at the couch, he knew he couldn't leave Willow there. The way she was sleeping would give her one hell of a neck cramp.

With a sigh, he picked her up and carried her back to the bedroom. In her sleep she moaned slightly and tried to snuggle closer to him.

I wonder what she's dreaming of. What, or who, can put that sweet smile on her face in sleep? Lovingly tucking a stray strand of hair behind her ear as he laid her down, Seth felt another surge of jealousy.

Gods, I need to get myself under control. Situating her into his bed, he watched, curious when she pouted and whimpered when he pulled away.

Returning to the kitchen, he grabbed the DVDs. After making sure all the curtains were pulled tightly shut and the doors locked, Seth settled down on the couch and began watching the first movie.

CB&O

Where am I? What's going on? Willow woke up disoriented. She could remember going to the bar, helping Seth and calling her sister. *How did I end up in a bed?*

Seth must have come back. Either that or Jason took pity on me. Of course if he moved me, I won't hear the end of it. Did Seth ever come back? Shaking her head she decided to simply be thankful she was still fully dressed.

Groggily, she climbed out of the bed and walked toward the living room, her bare feet carrying her through the apartment soundlessly.

When she saw Seth sitting on the couch watching a movie, she could only stop and stare. The dim light didn't conceal how handsome he was. Her body ached to go to him, to feel his arms around her again. Looking at the screen of the television, she tried to see what had him completely engrossed, what had him spellbound to the point he hadn't heard her approach.

After a few moments she recognized the movie. The horribly burned face would be almost impossible to not recognize.

She walked up behind him and stared in fascination at how absorbed he was in the story.

"Seth?" She called his name quietly, careful not to touch him. After all, she hated it when people snuck up on her while she was watching a horror movie and scared the bejeezus out of her.

He jumped up and jerked back as though the monster from the screen had come to life.

"I didn't mean to scare you. Why are you watching *Nightmare on Elm Street?*"

He didn't answer her immediately. Turning, he watched the screen for a few moments as the villain gave an evil laugh. "I wanted to hear the rhyme," he answered without looking at her.

"Rhyme?" Willow asked confused.

"Is that what you think of me? Do you see me as some monster who will invade your dreams and terrorize you?"

He sounded hurt, so lost. The conversation they had at the bar came flooding back to her. "Oh…" She didn't know what to say. Now that she'd gotten a decent night's sleep, she was thinking much clearer. She walked around the couch and sat on the opposite side of him. "Seth, I— I'm not sure what to think." She reached over and grabbed the remote, cutting the television off and forcing him to look at her. "What *am* I supposed to think of you? You are a complete contradiction. You give me the best sex of my life and make me think that you are at least part god, but then I find out you've been drinking my blood. Just taking something from me…"

"Would you have given me permission? Do you think you would have said 'No, I don't mind, drink all you want'?"

Willow shook her head. "I don't know what I would have said because I was never given the chance. I don't know, maybe I would have said 'go for it,' thinking it was some weird fetish, or you were just a freak. Maybe I would have said 'no way, no how,' and walked away. Maybe someday I'll be queen of the universe and all will bow before my glory. The point is you didn't have any right to make the decision for me."

"You're right, and it was wrong of me. But I'm not exactly accustomed to just telling everyone I know— women that I pick up in a bar—that I'm a vampire."

"I don't care what you do with everyone else!" She certainly didn't like hearing about him picking up other women. "I can forgive—hell, I can ignore the first time you did it. You didn't know me from Eve. I understand you wouldn't want your secret out. But after that, after you invited me to stay here with you, I had a right to know."

"What do you want me to say? You're right. And 'I'm sorry' doesn't begin to cover how I feel."

"But would you feel the same way if I hadn't found out your secret?" She stood and started to pace across the room. "Would you still be sitting here telling me how sorry you are if I hadn't run out of here?"

"I was planning on telling you. I was going to tell you the night you found out." He looked away from her.

"What happened?" she asked curiously, stepping closer.

"I was afraid you would run from me. That you would freak-out and run screaming from my apartment wearing nothing but what you had on at the time. I just wanted one more taste." He turned to look into her eyes. "I just needed one more taste of you, in case you decided to leave."

She was speechless. What could she say? She had reacted exactly as he believed she would when she found out the truth.

"I didn't know vampires' stomachs growled," she changed the subject.

"They don't."

"Then how...why... Now I'm confused." She sat back down on the couch, facing him.

Seth gave a bitter laugh. "Join the club, swe...Willow."

"You never answered my question earlier. Did you feed after I left?"

"Every night. More than once on some nights." He watched her as he spoke. Was he trying to gauge her reaction?

Willow felt an instant surge of anger rush up from his answer. She clenched her jaw to prevent herself from spitting an insult at him, reminding herself it was none of her business whom he "ate".

"But it didn't seem to matter," he continued. "No one satisfied me. No one was able to ease my thirst, my pain. No one, until you did last night."

"I don't care if they 'satisfied' you. It's none of my business what happened between you and your *donors*. It's not like I want every little detail," she replied cattily, trying to sound as if she didn't care about his answer.

Seth chuckled. "Feeding isn't something sexual unless I make it that way."

Willow sniffed in disbelief, her hand automatically covering the sore spot above her thigh. "You expect me to believe that you don't have sex with your donors? What, did I get 'stupid' tattooed across my forehead while I was asleep?"

"I didn't say that. Sex does make the blood sweeter. Compare it to a milkshake. The excess adrenaline is the ice cream—sweet and creamy. The orgasm acts like the whipped cream and together they slide down your throat, refreshing you, making you glad you indulged. The more powerful the orgasm, the more intoxicating the blood is."

"I really did not feel the need—or the desire—to know that. But thanks for sharing," she spit out sarcastically. "I'm gonna be really mad if I can't enjoy one of my favorite drinks anymore now that you've compared it to blood."

"Yes, I have drank from women after pleasuring them in bed. It was a give-take relationship. I gave them pleasure, and they gave me their blood."

"You mean you took their blood. Giving implies consent."

"Fine, I took their blood. The only side effect was they felt as though they had donated blood, which they had done, even if they didn't know about it. And I happen to believe my...method is more pleasant than someone jabbing your arm with a needle then just handing you a cookie and some juice."

"What exactly is the point here?" Willow asked irritably. She wasn't sure why, but the thought of him with all those other women, the way he dismissed having sex with countless other women, made her want to slap him. Hard. Possibly repeating the gesture until her hand hurt.

"The point, Willow, is that feeding is precisely that for me. Tell me, is there anything sexual to you about eating a slice of pizza?"

"Depends on how you eat it," she responded before she could stop herself.

"Exactly. You were the first woman who has ever experienced an orgasm simply from my bite."

"And why exactly do you think I care about that?" She tried to keep her voice neutral.

"I just know." She waited a second for him to expand on his answer, but he didn't.

"I don't know what you're talking about," she lied.

"There's nothing for you to be jealous of."

"Who says I'm jealous? I'm not jealous," she protested.

"Yes, you are. I can see it written all over you."

Chapter Ten

"While we're on the subject," she ignored his comment about her jealousy, "other than invading my dreams, what other mind games can you play?"

"Mind games?" Seth asked, confused.

"Yeah, mind games. You can enter my mind while I'm sleeping, can you enter while I'm awake? Can you read my thoughts?"

"Yes, I can look into your mind if I wish to. It's easier if we are both in the same room, but with enough concentration I can reach you anywhere."

"Because you drank from me?" She had a feeling that she already knew the answer to her question.

"No." He shook his head. "But it does make it much easier. It becomes easier still if you taste my blood."

"Are you reading my thoughts now?" Willow asked, clearly deciding to ignore the "drinking his blood" portion of the answer.

"No."

"Why should I believe you?"

"If I were reading your thoughts this conversation would be much easier." Seth laid his head back on the couch. "At least in your thoughts, I can understand the full context of what you're asking and give you a full answer."

"That was how you knew what my bathing suit looked like."

"Yes."

"If you're not reading my thoughts, why do you think I'm jealous?" she argued.

Seth turned his head to face her and opened his eyes. "Willow, if your jaw gets any tighter you might crack a tooth. And I'm pretty sure the pillow in your hands is about to rip. Unless, perhaps it has somehow found a way to annoy you?"

Looking down, she was surprised to see a small cream colored pillow in her hands. She couldn't remember picking it up. Her knuckles were white, and the fabric stretched so taut she was shocked it hadn't been shredded by her grip. Forcing herself to relax her hands, she put it down. "That still doesn't mean I'm jealous. It doesn't prove anything."

Seth gave her a pained but very patient look.

"I'm not jealous," she insisted. "Let's see, thus far we've established that you're a vampire, you can enter my dreams and read my thoughts, and feeding isn't sexual for you," she changed the subject again. She didn't like him thinking that she was jealous. Especially when she refused to admit she was feeling that way to herself. "Oh, and after you drank from me no other woman seemed to quite, 'satisfy' you."

"Yes." He agreed without moving.

"What else do I need to know?"

"What else would you like to know?"

"Do I have to go get tested? Do vampires get STDs?"

"No," he chuckled. "There is no blood disease in existence that can harm us. Something about the way our bodies process blood."

"What about pregnancy? Is there a chance you could have gotten me pregnant?"

"Yes. But," he added quickly before she could begin to panic, "it is very hard for my people and full humans to have a child. Statistically, it's almost impossible."

"Almost impossible. That's different from impossible. It means there is still a chance. Okay, that's fine, I'll just ride it out. No need to panic and scare myself yet... When did you die?"

"I'm sorry? Could you repeat the last question?" Seth jerked his head up from the back of the couch where it had been resting.

"Is it a sensitive subject? It's alright if you don't want to talk about it. Of course it's on the weird side, and if I stop to think about it I might start to freak again. I'm sure I'll get over it eventually... I just never imagined I'd be into necrophilia..."

"I. Am. Not. Dead. Do I look dead? Do I feel dead? By the old gods, why do you think I'm dead?"

"Vampires are always dead. That's how they're made. It's what all the books and shows say..." Her voice trailed off as she confessed her source of information.

"And once again, pop culture misses the truth. I did not die. I was not turned into a vampire. I was born a vampire. I've always been a vampire."

"When were you born?"

"Eight hundred years ago."

"Wow. You're old! Way old...older than old... At least you do look good for your age," she complimented him, her gaze traveling over his body. "Very good..."

"Thank you," he answered tersely.

"Can you eat? I mean other than blood?"

"Yes. I happen to find some foods very pleasing, but it's not necessary. My body gains no nourishment from regular foods, though sometimes I do have a sweet tooth. How exactly is this helping you?" He sounded curious and somewhat annoyed. Willow guessed it was the whole "when did you die" question. Maybe she'd struck a nerve.

"It just is. And you aren't sure what it means that your body only seems to want my blood? Why my blood? What's special about it? More importantly, what will happen to you if I walk out that door and never look back?"

"I'm not sure," he lied. Seth closed his eyes and leaned his head back once more. "I don't know why my body won't accept any other blood and I can only guess what would happen to me. I believe one of two things will happen. The first guess is that if I can allow myself to

176

become hungry enough I might be able to break past whatever is stopping me from gaining nourishment elsewhere. But then I also run the risk of draining whomever I drink from, unable to stop myself in my hunger."

"Or," she prompted. She wasn't sure why, but she didn't quite buy his answer. There was something about the way he refused to look her in the eye, the way he was avoiding looking at her altogether.

"Or, I'll starve to death." He said it without being condescending, as if he were merely discussing cold facts instead of his life.

"Basically, you're telling me if I walk away I'll kill you?"

"We don't know that..." He hadn't moved. Seth kept his head resting against the back of the couch as though they were discussing something of little importance rather than his life.

"Seth, don't lie to me. At least pretend you have more respect for me than that. Treat me like I was something more than just a free meal or two."

Seth lifted his head and stared into her face. "Fine. Does it make you feel better to know that I know if you walk away I will die? That I will slowly starve to death because no other blood will ease my hunger? I'm prepared to accept my fate."

"But... I could..." Her heart wrenched at the thought of losing him.

"No. Don't even think about it," he snarled. "I won't let you stay in my life because you feel an obligation to me. I'd rather be dead than know the only reason you're here is to feed me."

"Seth..."

"No. That is not negotiable, Willow."

"And just how do you plan on stopping me if that's what I decide to do?" she asked, her tone growing harsh to match his.

"Simple, I'll refuse to drink."

"Yeah, because it worked so well last time you tried to refuse me, right?" She was too angry to worry about blushing over the memory of how she'd enticed him to drink.

"Why do you care?" he roared. "I'm nothing more than a monster to you. Why do you care if I live or die? You walked out on me. You can't do that then just pretend like everything is fine. I won't let you stomp all over my poor 'undead' heart again."

"What?" She wasn't sure she'd heard him correctly.

"Nothing." He stormed out of the room.

Willow followed him into the kitchen. She couldn't have heard him correctly, right? *I stomped on his heart?*

Seth gestured to the pile of chocolate on the counter. "If you still want chocolate, I grabbed plenty. I wasn't sure what you liked..."

"Whoa, back up there, vamp-boy. Did you say you won't let me stomp all over your heart again? As in, I've already stomped on it once?"

"Does it matter?" He played with a chocolate bar and refused to look at her.

"I do care. I don't know why. God knows I don't understand it. But seeing you so weak last night, knowing that you needed help... I couldn't just walk away."

"Great. Just what every man wants to hear." Sarcasm dripped from his every word. "I don't want your pity. Don't worry about me, I've survived for eight hundred years without you in my life, I'm sure I'll be just fine after you leave. And I assure you, now that I know precisely how you feel, I will not 'terrorize' your dreams any longer." Seth turned and walked away from her again.

This time Willow didn't follow him. She grabbed one of the chocolate bars and made her way to the elevator. There was too much to think about right now. She needed some time and space to consider what she had learned. And something deep inside her insisted Seth needed some space as well.

With an oddly heavy heart, Willow pressed the lobby button. This time, before she left the building she grabbed a business card giving the address, just in case she decided to try to check on Seth.

Climbing inside a taxi, she kept the card firmly inside her hand instead of placing it in her pocket.

When they arrived at her building, she was thankful that she'd worn jeans and remembered to take money with her. After paying the driver, she hurried to her apartment, lost in her own thoughts.

When Roxy opened the door, Willow surprised her sister by simply walking past her, ignoring all of her questions. She strode to her bedroom and shut the door, locking it just to be sure Roxy didn't barge in.

Seconds later she was glad she'd taken the time to turn the lock as her sister banged on the door. "Willow! Open this door this minute. Tell me what is going on right now." Roxy kept demanding answers as she hammered on Willow's door as though she were trying to break it down.

Taking her cue from Seth's behavior earlier, Willow shouted, "Leave me the hell alone."

She knew her sister wouldn't be prepared for her anger, but she needed time to herself to decide what she wanted. She was right, almost instantly the pounding stopped.

Willow paced inside the room like a caged animal, questions and feelings almost overwhelming her.

Can I be with a man who only sees me as a meal? Dinner and dessert, anytime he wants it?

But does he just feel that way about me? He wouldn't have made the "stomp all over his heart comment" if I was just a walking buffet, would he?

But won't a man—vampire—whatever, say anything he needs to if he isn't ready to die?

Could we just be friends? I could just let him drink from me every few days... We could just become best friends...

Willow couldn't even convince herself of the plausibility of that last thought. She could never handle watching him smile and flirt with another woman.

Unable to handle her rampant thoughts any longer, Willow lay on her bed. Even terrified Seth would come to her in her dreams again, she'd still felt comfort in being able to sleep. She may have limited how much sleep she allowed herself, but there was a small amount of comfort in the knowledge that there was a chance he would come to her, that he would hold her.

As she lay in the bed now, Willow couldn't help but shudder. The thought of sleep no longer comforted her. He'd promised he would never enter her dreams again. Without any chance of seeing him again, sleeping seemed a bleak and hopeless action. She wondered if she could try to find him, if their connection was a two-way deal.

Clinging to that tiny thread of hope, Willow closed her eyes and drifted off into sleep.

CB⬥EO

Seth could feel the slight tug on their connection as he stared out his bedroom window. He didn't see the twinkling lights or traffic, he saw Willow, her body uncovered for him. One minute she was lying tantalizingly on his bed, in a pose that threatened every ounce of self-control he could ever remember possessing. The next, she was straddling his chest, begging him to bite her.

He felt his teeth lengthen as his mouth watered at the view she presented him with. Memories of the show she put on for him had his cock hard and flexing beneath his pants.

How many women would tease their men the way Willow teased me?

Did Willow tease other men the same way?

Seth's fists clenched and he had to back away from the window to prevent himself from smashing it. Reluctantly he admitted that taking his anger out on the glass would do no good. *It won't make me feel better and it sure as hell won't bring Willow back. All it will do is make a mess and allow the sun's rays to enter the room.*

Perhaps that would be for the best? If I'm not here, she won't be tempted to sacrifice any possible happiness she could have simply to keep me alive...

Shaking his head, he forced himself to walk away from the temptation. He would follow the bedtime story his mother told him. He would take a few days to get his possessions in order. He would leave notes for his family, and for Jason. His friend deserved to know why he had chosen the path that he did. Then, just before the hunger became unbearable, he would take the honorable way out. The only way that would guarantee no innocent people would be harmed. He would watch the sun rise.

Comforted by his decision, Seth stripped and climbed into his bed. He took a deep breath, breathing in Willow's scent as it clung to his sheets, his pillow.

There was another tug on their connection. Turning away from it, he ignored it. He had given his word that he would never terrorize her dreams again, and he would keep his promise. *It's only wishful thinking,* he tried to convince himself. *Why would she want to see me again?* As he closed his eyes, he remembered the monster she had compared him to. He could hear the evil laugh of that horribly scarred man taunting him.

CRECO

"Roxy, I'm going out," Willow called as she tried to hurry out of the door before her sister could stop her.

"Where are you going? You've gone out the last three nights straight. What happened to you, Will? First you're depressed and won't leave the apartment then you disappear and lock yourself in your room for two nights. When you finally do come out, you spend all night somewhere, not coming home until dawn. Sis, I'm getting worried."

"I'm fine. At least, I think I am. I just needed to work through something," Willow told Roxy honestly.

"And now you have?"

"Yes. Now I have." For two days and nights she'd refused all contact with people, concentrating only on Seth. She'd tried to contact him, tried to figure out what she wanted. Anytime she tried to imagine her life without him, her stomach would clench into knots.

She still wasn't sure exactly what she felt for him, but she knew she wanted to at least give it—give them—a chance. She had thought and rethought her reasons until she was positive she wasn't doing anything simply because she felt an obligation to him. But Willow also wanted to make sure she was more than a pet to him. She couldn't be that. Not even if she were treated as a prized pet and given anything she ever desired in exchange for the blood she provided.

As she tried to make her decision, her thoughts continuously returned to the week she'd spent with Seth. At no time while she was there had he made her feel like anything but a welcome guest. Looking back, now that she knew he'd drank her blood, she still couldn't detect any difference in how'd he treated her.

"What do you do every night, Will?" Roxy's voice pulled her out of her thoughts again. "You leave at sunset and don't come back until nearly dawn. What are you doing?"

"I'm looking for someone." Willow answered her sister's question, knowing Roxy wouldn't give up until she had at least a few answers.

Roxy shot her a disbelieving look. "It doesn't take *that* long to find someone."

"It does when you're looking for someone specific but you don't know where to find him. And if you'll excuse me, I have to go. I'm going to be unbelievably pissed at you if you make me miss my meeting." Without another word, Willow turned and left the apartment.

She could barely contain her excitement when she reached the bar. It had taken two nights, but she'd finally gotten the bartender to talk to her. He'd sworn to her that Jason would be in tonight, but he wasn't sure what time. He'd explained the man was scheduled for an update, that he would be there—even if just for a few minutes—to make sure everything was running smoothly while Seth was unavailable.

Walking in, she panicked. What if she had missed him? When the bartender saw her approach, he smiled and shook his head. He reassured her that she hadn't missed Jason.

Willow sat at a table, careful to face the door. She also made certain to keep a lazy eye on the bar, thankful for the peaceful crowd. Since the Night Crawlers weren't due to play until the next night, Willow felt reasonably sure she would be able to spot Jason as soon as he walked in.

Dismissing all the men asking her to dance and denying anyone who asked to join her, Willow tried to wait patiently, constantly reminding herself that the bartender said she hadn't missed him. After what felt like an eternity, Jason finally arrived.

Willow watched him enter and stride over to the bar. His blond hair made him easier to pick out in the dim lighting. She waited for Jason to speak to the bartender, before leaving her table to approach him as he lounged against the polished countertop. She had a favor to ask and didn't want to piss him off by interrupting his business.

She was only a few feet away from him when Jason turned and stared at her.

"Can we talk?"

"I'm pretty busy right now," Jason told her coldly.

"Please. Just five minutes." She used the same line he had when he approached her about Seth.

"Make it quick," he sighed, repeating her answer.

"Can we at least go sit down?"

Jason nodded and followed Willow to her table.

"It's about Seth..." she began timidly.

"Go on." His voice was unemotional as he sat opposite her.

"I want you to take me to him."

"Why?" He leaned forward. She seemed to have his undivided attention now.

"I tried to go see him a few nights ago..." She paused, uncertain how much to tell him. "I had his address, but couldn't get up to his apartment. And when I spoke to the manager, he said that Seth wouldn't pick up his phone. Without Seth's approval, my hands are tied. I couldn't even get the number of the floor he lives on or his phone number." And damn her sister—Roxy had erased the number off their caller ID.

Jason nodded. "Seth's very particular about his privacy. He makes certain his managers are quite aware of that. I'm sure you can understand why."

"Just take me to him. That's all I want. All I'm asking you for."

Jason snorted. "Why should I? Are you planning on killing him this time? At least then he'd be put out of his misery. Do you know what it feels like to starve to death?" His tone became nasty.

"Listen to me, sport," she said, getting nasty right back. "I only want a few minutes of his time. I need to talk to him and don't ask me what I want to talk to him about. Because it's none of your business." Willow's temper was rising, getting the best of her good intentions to play nice.

"Then you damn sure aren't getting taken to his apartment," Jason stated as he leaned back. He crossed his arms over his chest, and glared at her. "Do you know what I had to go through to find out what was going on with him? To get him to tell me that he was slowly dying? He's the best friend I've ever had and I will not let you hurt him, again."

After a minute she gave up. She could understand his concern. "Fine. Look, I needed a few days to work through everything. I don't think it was too much to ask for considering all the information that was thrown at me. And your friend made it pretty clear he didn't want me around at that moment as well." Her tone softened, became almost pleading. "I just want to tell him what I decided. And I want to tell him in person—in private. I don't think that's too much to ask for either."

"Fine." Jason stood. "Why not, I don't think you could put him in a worse mood." Without looking back to see if she was following, he walked through the bar to the exit.

Five very tense minutes later she was in the elevator with Jason, heading up to see Seth.

When the doors opened Willow stepped out and Jason gave a slight bow, a sarcastic smile on his face. As the doors closed once more, leaving her alone in the apartment, she wondered if she'd made the right decision.

"Seth?" Walking through the apartment, she called out his name, looking for him. The bedroom door loomed before her and she felt another moment of doubt.

"Seth?" She called him again as she knocked. When he didn't answer, she opened the door, gasping at the mess she saw.

"Oh my God," she exclaimed as she looked around. Clothes and glass were all over the floor. Anything fragile had been broken, and over half of the material on the floor was shredded.

"What do you want?" he growled from the side of the room.

"Seth? What happened?" At first she didn't see him. When she spotted his form squatting in a corner, she rushed toward him.

"Go away, Willow." He turned away from her, showing her his back.

"What's wrong, what's going on?" Concern flooded her body. Reaching out, she moved forward until she was only a few feet shy of touching him. Moving slowly so she didn't startle him, she continued to close the distance between them.

"Go away," he screamed, still in the corner.

"No. Let me help you..." Before she could say another word he was standing. He moved forward, pushing her back against the wall.

"You want to help me? Leave. Me. Alone. Walk away while you still can, before I forget that I'm not the monster all those stories claim I am." He leaned in close to her neck and took a deep breath. "Gods, you smell so sweet." He growled again

"Seth..." Willow stroked his cheek gently.

"Don't touch me." He pulled away as if her touch were painful. As though she had burned him. He flew to the other side of the room almost faster than her gaze could follow. "Say what you came to say then leave me alone."

Willow was stunned. This man was different from the gentle lover she had known, different from the sad man she had seen less than a week before. "What happened to you?"

Seth was practically shaking with need. He needed to feel her wrapped around him, needed to taste her beneath his lips, needed her blood to finally ease the beast roaring in pain and hunger within him.

But more than anything he needed her to leave. He would not allow her to become a sacrificial lamb, to be around him because she pitied him. And he wasn't sure how much longer he could keep his growing hunger at bay. *And by the old gods, I will not hurt her like* that. He could smell her skin, the lotion she used. It only served to make him hungrier. He knew, as he was now, he could never be gentle with her.

"You happened," he snapped. It was better to hurt her feelings than risk her life, her chance at happiness.

"Me?"

"Yes, you. You walked into my life and turned everything upside down. I was hoping that I would never have to see you again after you left the last time, but I can see I have to be blunt. Leave. Don't come back. You should have taken the hint when my managers refused to help you." He forced a nasty laugh out of his mouth, ignoring the bad taste it left. "What, you thought I didn't know about that? I knew. I knew you wanted to see me, but I didn't want to see you. But you just wouldn't take the hint. Now I'm telling you to leave me alone. Do not try to come up to my apartment again. Don't try to call me. Don't try to contact me in any way."

"Seth..." The sadness in her voice was ripping him apart bit by bit. It was somehow worse than the hunger.

"Leave," he roared. *Please,* he begged the gods, *please let her leave. I don't know how much longer I can be strong and do what's right.*

Without another word she turned and walked out of the room.

Alone with his anger and hunger once more, Seth slid down the wall to the floor. His only chance for happiness had just walked out of his life for the third, and hopefully final, time.

He cradled his head and tried to block out the faint traces of her scent that even now lingered in the room, teasing him.

Chapter Eleven

Willow pushed the button and waited for the elevator to arrive.

He doesn't want me... Her heart shattered. *After all that, he doesn't want me.*

She was stunned. Never once had she believed he would dismiss her like that. She could almost hear violin music playing inside her head as she threw herself a pity party.

Snap out of it, an angry voice inside her said roughly. *After everything you went through to get here, to be able to talk to him and tell him what you want, you're just going to walk away without saying a word? Grow a backbone! You don't deserve to be happy if you won't stand up for yourself!*

And now you have your answer, don't you? It's good to finally know that you really were just going to be with him out of obligation, the voice taunted. *We should be grateful; he saved you from one giant mistake.*

No, she screamed back. *I'm not here because of any obligation. I went through all that trouble because I wanted, needed, to see him again.*

Yeah, right, and when did the sky turn green? If you were serious about it, about him, you would not have just walked out again. You fight for things you want, you don't turn around and just stroll away from them. Never once have you walked away from something you truly wanted.

Stop it. He doesn't want me here. A tear ran down her cheek.

So what? I guess it is easier to take; to simply walk away and not risk having your feelings be trampled on than to actually fight for him.

He's already trampled them, she argued.

And still you didn't say one word. Roxy's right, you do give up on things too easily. No wonder you couldn't hack it at your job, no wonder you got fired. You weren't willing to fight for your reputation, why should you fight for a man you claim you care for?

Willow snapped her head up. She cared about Seth. No, that wasn't right. Roxy had been right that first night I was home, after I found out the truth about Seth. Somehow, someway, she had already fallen in love with him. She loved his sense of adventure, his sense of humor. She loved the way he was always touching her, as if he couldn't get enough. She loved his compassion and his giant ego. And she loved who she was when she was with him. The way she felt whole and completely accepted.

She had fallen in love with him. Why else would his pain cause her such grief?

"Fine, I'll fight," she told herself. "I'm not leaving this apartment until I've at least admitted the truth to him."

The elevator doors opened but she just turned around and strode back toward his bedroom, embracing her anger. She allowed it to strengthen her for the heart-wrenching scene she knew would be behind the door. He didn't want her? Fine, but like it or not he would hear what she had to say. He would not dismiss her again until she said what she had come here to say, damn it.

This time she didn't bother to knock, she simply opened the door and strode in, ignoring the mess.

"You listen to me, fang-boy, I'm not leaving until I say what I came here to say." She stood in the doorway, her hands on her hips and filled with indignation. "I didn't go through all the trouble I've gone through simply to get into your apartment out of obligation. Yes, I freaked out when I found out you were a vampire. Big deal. Any woman would have. Whether it was on the first night or five years from now, it wasn't something I ever expected to hear. And yes, I left the second time. But you made it clear to me that you didn't want me here. You wouldn't listen when I tried to tell you I wasn't calling you Freddy. I was scared, damn it. I was scared and tired and I needed to figure out what I wanted. And I did—I have. I know exactly what I want and I am not leaving here until you know what I want too.

"If I thought of you as a monster I wouldn't have looked back after I left. I wouldn't have cared if you were in pain. But I did. God knows I didn't want to. I wanted to run. I wanted to be able to walk away and not look back, but I couldn't, because for some reason it *mattered* to me that you were hurting. I couldn't walk away. But that didn't mean I wasn't still scared and confused. And then I was even more scared and confused because I realized I *did* care what happened to you.

"I went through the trouble to find you to tell you that I wanted us to try and figure out what there is between us. I'm not here to promise to become your willing buffet—but I was here to ask for a chance. I haven't been able to stop thinking about you. I dream of you. Not because you are invading my dreams. I know you aren't because it doesn't feel quite as real when you hold me in these dreams. I dream of you because I care. I may not be the sharpest tool in the shed, but I did finally figure it out.

"I am imperfect and full of flaws," she admitted. "God, I'm standing here screaming at a vampire who right now is probably capable of killing me without any remorse. You're so hungry you could probably drain me dry before you realized what you'd done, but here I am.

"You want me to leave, fine. I'll leave. I won't bother you ever again. But I will not allow you sit there and blame me for what's happening to you. I will not let you go on thinking 'oh poor me, she's only here because she thinks she has to be'. I'm here because at some point I fell in love with your sorry ass and for the life of me, now I cannot figure out why, because you're nothing more than some...some jerk with an..." Willow hesitated. Who could she compare him to? An image of the broody vampire from one of her favorite television shows popped into her mind. "...Angel complex. Don't even try to pretend you are perfect either, it's not like you don't have flaws Mr. 'Keep-a-girl-around-for-a-handy-snack'."

Willow cleared her throat uncertainly. "The screaming portion of tonight is now over, and, I'll admit it sounded better in my head. How can you expect me to ball you out when you're sitting there looking pathetic? You know what, I'm leaving. It's obvious you don't want me here, and I won't force myself on you. There was no way I was going to leave and let you have your nice little pity party without saying what I wanted to say. What I went through so much trouble to be able to say to you."

Willow turned and stormed back to the door. Before she could get there, Seth was in front of her.

"Say it again," he whispered.

"Which part, the part where I called you a jerk or the part where I told you that you were acting like a baby? she asked irritably. "Do you have to do the super-speed thing?"

His expression was so hopeful Willow felt her anger melting away. "Tell me the part where you said you cared, that you loved me."

"If you don't believe me, look for yourself," she offered, her tone much more gentle than before. "Look inside my mind. Tell me what you see."

She watched as Seth closed his eyes. As with the biting, now that she knew what he was doing she could almost feel the caress of his mind as he looked into her thoughts. She tried to hold nothing back, to let him see just what she felt, but wasn't sure if what she did worked.

She could see the shock all over his face, but it was intensified when he opened his eyes. He looked as though he were afraid to believe her.

Tenderly he reached up and cupped her cheek.

"Willow..." he began but stopped, his voice sounding hoarse.

"I'm here because I want to be here. I want to be with you. I won't lie, it took a little time to get used to the thought of you drinking my blood. But I came to realize that's only a part of who you are. Seth, no man has ever made me feel anywhere near the way I feel when I'm with you. If you want me to leave, I will. But you can not force me to stop caring about you. No matter how mean you are, no matter how much you try to hurt me. Not even by doing something stupid like trying to sacrifice yourself from a future you don't believe I want."

"Gods, Willow." Seth shook his head and began to sway.

"Let's get you to the bed. And don't argue with me," she ordered.

Placing his arm around her shoulders, Willow circled her arm around his waist. Slowly they inched toward the bed. She knew he wasn't really leaning on her, but didn't try to press the issue, as they made their progress.

She watched him sway as he tried to keep his balance while she swept the clothes and other various items lying on top of it to the floor.

"Lay down," she ordered. Without a second thought, she climbed on the mattress and lay beside him. "You need to eat something."

Seth shook his head. "I won't let you do this," he protested.

"Seth, honey, please, don't make me force you. I have to admit it was nice, but quite honestly I'm not sure I'm up for it right now. But I will if I have to. Please," she tilted her head and exposed the side of her neck closest to him. "I want to feel your lips on me," she whispered. "I want to feel you inside of me."

She watched him lean down. Gently nibbling on her neck, it was as though he couldn't refuse her. Closing her eyes, Willow braced herself, unsure of what exactly to expect. Whatever it was, she didn't feel anything. Looking at him, she saw him tilt his head gently to the side.

She couldn't stop the sound she made when his lips descended on hers as he kissed her tenderly. He slid his tongue into her mouth, playing with hers as he shifted a hand to tease her breast. He kissed a path down her cheek to her neck, then to the sensitive spot near the base.

"Are you sure?" he breathed across her flesh after his tongue swirled around the pulse.

Nodding, Willow felt her heartbeat speed up. Excitement filled her as her feelings rose from deep within.

She felt his teeth slide into her skin as soon as she gave her consent. She was taken by surprise when there was no pain. When he began to gently suckle on her neck, all thoughts ceased and she couldn't do anything but feel.

How can he say this isn't sexual? she wondered as her entire body came to life from the simple gesture.

"With you in my arms, Willow, breathing almost becomes a sensual pleasure for me," he responded.

It took a moment for her pleasure-fogged mind to realize he hadn't spoken out loud, that his lips were still on her neck.

"Seth," she moaned.

"Yes, Willow?"

"You can call me sweetheart," she responded breathlessly.

"Only sweetheart?" His voice was teasing.

"What else—what else did you have—have in mind," she stammered as the fire in her blood became hotter, more consuming.

"Mmmmmm," he moaned in her head. *"Sweetheart. My Love. Mate. Wife?"*

Willow was so caught up in the sensations completely surrounding her that she missed his question. Her body was close to a mind-shattering orgasm, she could almost feel him buried inside her. Her body was about to explode when he eased his teeth from her flesh and his tongue slid over the wound. She was amazed at how empty, how alone she felt now that he had withdrawn from her.

"Are you sure you aren't some form of drug?" Willow asked as she jerked at his shirt. "Because I think I'm addicted to you."

"No, sweetheart. But you are," he said before kissing her.

Seth pulled on her clothing. In no time, the items were lying in a pile, ripped beyond repair as his quickly followed in much the same condition.

He lowered his head to tease her nipple but she yanked his head up to her mouth. "No. I need you now. You can play later. I'll go insane if I don't feel you inside me right now."

Seth stroked down her body, his hands rubbing every inch of her flesh until he reached her sex. He slid a finger deep inside her, causing her to whimper and raise her hips, trying to take him deeper. "Gods, you're wet already," he moaned. With one quick motion he was between her legs and buried deep inside her.

Their loving was fast and hard, and after just a few strokes both were shouting with ecstasy as they came together.

Without separating them, Seth rolled onto his back. Once there, he rubbed her body from neck to ass.

Willow lay contentedly for a few moments, basking in the pleasure she'd just experienced. She gloried in smelling him beneath her, on her skin, feeling his arms wrapped tightly around her.

Suddenly, what he'd whispered into her mind as he drank from her clicked. Lifting her head she said, "Wait a second, back up there, Fangy, did you just ask me to marry you?"

"I was wondering if you caught that." He smiled.

"Hey, it took a few minutes to process it. I was more than a little distracted you know," she threw back. Her voice became more gentle. "Did you mean it?"

"With all my heart." He stared into her eyes.

"See, now look what you did. Now I'm gonna cry..." Tears of happiness welled up in her eyes.

"I'm sorry, we don't have to get married if you don't want to." She knew he was trying his best to comfort her.

"Listen here tall, dark and toothy, if you take that proposal back I'm going to break every window in this apartment, rip down all the curtains and bake your ass in the sunlight."

Seth chuckled. "Then I guess that means you want to marry me?"

"Yes I do, vamp-boy." She snuggled into his chest.

"Vamp-boy, fangy, fang-boy, tall, dark and toothy, what's next? Bloodsucker?" She knew from his tone that he was teasing her.

"I'm just trying to find a nickname I like..." She purred as his hands ceased to be comforting and began arousing her.

"I draw the line at Dracula. That cousin of mine caused more trouble..." Seth looked at her and chuckled. "Long story, one I promise I'll tell you...another time.

Sandy Lynn

What about my lord or prince of pleasure or, oh, master of my heart? I like that one. It has a nice ring to it."

Willow laughed. "In your dreams. How about I just call you mine?"

"That will definitely work for me," Seth smiled.

"Seth," Willow began seriously, her tone stopping his hands. "Will you make me like you? Will you turn me into a vampire so we can always be together?" Her voice was just above a whisper.

"If that is what you want." He pulled her head back down to his chest, comforting her again.

"And if I don't want to be a vampire? I don't want to die," she confessed. "Even if I do come right back..."

"I told you, sweetheart, we aren't dead. There is another option," he began. "But it's a little more...complex. We don't have to discuss this now..." His voice trailed off.

"Will you tell me?"

"I've heard of another way, but only in stories. I've never actually known anyone that used the process. Typically people simply become vampires... But that doesn't mean they die," he quickly added again. "Think of becoming a vampire as more of a blood transfusion. You would be given my blood in growing quantities every few days until you were changed," he explained.

"What about your need for my blood?"

202

"That will always be there, whether you remain human or become a vampire. But if you change, we will both need to drink from others for our...nourishment."

"What's the other way?"

"You still have to drink my blood. Only once every month or so, and in smaller quantities, but you'd have to do it for the rest of your life."

"How long would that be?"

"Barring a fatal wound, you would live as long as I do. You would never grow old. My blood has regenerative properties which will stop you from aging and prevent you from catching most diseases. It would also change your body. You'd become more light-sensitive and your senses would become more acute, but not noticeably so. It would change you just enough to increase the chances of us having a child, if you want one."

"Would I get fangs like yours?" She allowed one finger to stroke his lips, then slide down his mouth as if she were stroking his fang.

"I'm not sure."

"Why isn't it done more often? Why have you only heard about it being done in stories?" Willow raised her head and looked at him.

"You ask a lot of questions, sweetheart," he teased before answering her. "Honestly, I'm not sure. Maybe people weren't told it was an option... Maybe they didn't believe the stories. But if the Blood Mate story is true, I have no reason to doubt that another one would be equally true."

"Would you mind if we did that one? That choice?" She looked deep into his eyes.

"Not at all, sweetheart." He gave her a brief kiss. "We can do whatever you want, whenever you're ready. We have all the time in the world."

"To your people, what would I be called? Wife? Mate? Donor?"

"I have to call my mom to be sure, but, in the stories they were called Blood Mates." He nuzzled her neck, then scraped his sharp teeth over her flesh.

"Hungry again?" She chuckled.

"For you, sweetheart, always." He nibbled on her ear.

"Wait, did you say mother?" She grew nervous.

"Caught that, did you?" He was teasing her again.

"Does this mean I have to meet your family? How big is your family? Do I just meet your mom, or do I have to meet all of them? Oh God, what if they don't like me? What if we don't get along? What if your family and my family don't get along?"

"They are going to love you. And don't worry, I'm sure Roxy will grow on us all."

She smacked his arm. "But what if they don't? I mean, I'm sure I'm not at all what they expected. Do you have brothers and sisters? How many? You're not what Roxy expected either, you know. Will they all be able to read my mind? How many people are we talking about, Seth?"

He sighed. "Well, I guess it depends. Are we counting aunts, uncles and cousins as well?"

"Yes. No. Yes. Just tell me."

He kissed her gently on the lips. "Counting aunts, uncles and cousins, there were I believe three hundred at the last count. But you'll probably never meet a couple of them."

If her questions were any indication, her thoughts were flying all over the place. Before Jason came into his life, he'd have never been able to keep up with her—or understand her. No one else in Jason's family had ever prepared him for such a quirky woman. He would have to remember to thank his friend for getting him ready for his mate.

"Three hundred! Wait, why won't I get to meet them all?"

"Well, a few of them are...grounded, for lack of a better word."

"Vampires can get grounded?"

"They can when their mom finds out they've been boasting to humans again. Of course the real trouble happened when my aunt found out that one of the humans who heard my cousin's exaggerated boasts decided to write the story down and sell it as a book."

Her eyes widened. "Who?"

"My cousin, Vlad."

If possible, her eyes grew wider. "You mean, he...*the* Vlad is your cousin? *That* Vlad?"

"Don't believe everything you read in a book, love. Almost every word he said to that old hack was a lie. Pure fantasy. But a little thing like that didn't stop people from hunting us."

"Okay, I was nervous before, but now... You're family is famous. You—I..."

"Willow," Seth interrupted.

"Yes, Seth?" She was clearly distracted by his revelations.

"You're thinking too much."

"Then help me to stop." She lowered her head to his for a kiss.

"That, love, will be my pleasure." He still felt hungry, still had the desire to drink from her, but the aching pain had ceased. And now that he knew he had an eternity to be with her, to taste and love her, his hunger seemed to ease.

Chapter Twelve

Willow smiled as she watched Seth bring in the final boxes of her clothes.

"I don't think your sister likes me very much," he grumbled, remembering the way Roxy had yelled at him.

"Of course she doesn't. She's scared you're going to break my heart. You should have heard what she had to say when she found out I was moving in with you. She's not going to believe that you proposed until she sees us actually getting married. She warned me that I was making a mistake," Willow said, clearly enjoying being able to tease him. "And she couldn't believe I wouldn't take my job back. She wanted to know how you got my boss to admit he was lying."

"What did you tell her?"

"I told her you showed him your teeth," she teased again.

"Willow..." He scolded her menacingly, giving a mock growl.

"She thinks I was joking, calm down." Putting the box in her arms down, she approached him. "I have a surprise for you."

"You are all the surprise I could ever need." Leaning down he kissed her lips tenderly.

"Then does that mean you don't want to know what it is?"

"Hell no," he laughed.

To his delight, Willow echoed the sound, giving the throaty laugh he loved. "You have to catch me first." Without looking back at him, she turned and ran down the hall.

Looking at the box in his hands he smiled as he dropped it and easily caught up to her. Scooping her up into his arms, he carried her into their bedroom. No matter how many times he thought it, he couldn't stop the smile that came to his face when that phrase came up. Their room. He wasn't alone any more.

"No fair, you cheated."

"Haven't you heard, all's fair in love, sweetheart."

"Yeah, but you used your superpowers. And I don't have any." She pouted in his arms but didn't struggle to remove herself from his embrace.

Seth had to fight to repress his chuckle. He knew she was only teasing. "Now that just isn't true. You have much more power than I do," he said, playing along.

"I do? What powers?" Her hands rested lightly on the back of his neck, her fingers playing with his hair.

"Well, you have total and complete power over my heart."

"Good answer." Leaning in, she rested her head on his chest.

"Penny for your thoughts. No, wait, that'd be wrong. Kiss for your thoughts?"

"Just thinking. I did have to finally fess up about what you were wearing at the bar that first night."

"I always thought ladies didn't play kiss and tell."

"Yeah, but it's one of the rules. And well, I didn't tell them everything that happened between us."

Even through his shirt he could feel her face heat up. "Anything else?"

"Yes. I was wondering how fast we could get these clothes off—without ruining them, Seth—so you could make love to me."

That was all the invitation he needed. In one smooth motion he managed to pull her shirt off and lower his mouth to hers. As his tongue delved into her mouth, he freed her breasts. Ending the kiss, he helped her stand. Lowering the blasted jeans she insisted on wearing, he paused to place a tender kiss on her hip a second before he started nibbling on it. He smiled against her flesh as her hands twisted in his hair.

Pulling her back to his lap, Seth removed the rest of her clothing, pausing only when she tugged on his shirt. Standing, he tore away at his own pants, uncaring if they were destroyed. They were ruined for a good cause. Willow joined him, her hands resting on his chest. Picking her up, he laid her gently on the bed before lying down beside her and kissing her deeply. His tongue thrust into her mouth, an imitation of what his body was screaming it wanted. He didn't stop until she was moaning beneath him.

Lifting his head from her body, he ignored her whimpers. Tracing a trail down to her breast with his tongue, he teased her nipple, allowing his teeth to lengthen and graze against the tight bud before his tongue swirled around it.

Her hiss of pleasure was the only encouragement he needed to continue.

He trailed kisses between her breasts, over to the other nipple, teasing it while his hand stroked then raised her leg. As he suckled on her, his thumb delved between her folds, circling and teasing her clit. Within minutes she was writhing beneath his hands and mouth. When his finger slid inside her, Willow arched her neck and back, trying to get closer to him. He teased her, bringing her body close to orgasm then slowing his movements, prolonging the moment, the torture.

Pulling his finger out, he slid his cock into her, holding himself still once he was buried deep inside, driving her crazy. He knew she was close, that his entry had nearly caused her to orgasm.

Clawing at his back, she tried to entice him to move, but he remained frozen, once again denying her orgasm.

When he finally began to thrust, he was slow and gentle. "What's the rush, sweetheart? We have all night," he whispered against her mouth. Hell they had all eternity.

As their pleasure began to increase, Seth didn't try to hide the slight changes in him. He'd been surprised to discover that the subtle changes actually seemed to arouse his mate rather than repulse her. She seemed to revel in making him lose control. And he loved seeing that wild side of her.

Willow ran her tongue over his teeth, causing them to lengthen and sharpen as he kissed her then nibbled on her neck. Seth's teeth slid easily into her flesh as he took a quick sip of her blood then closed the wound.

"You are so addictive," he murmured against her flesh. "Gods, how am I supposed to control myself around you?"

Tangling her hands into his hair, she tugged until he was looking into her eyes.

"I want to taste you."

"Sweetheart, as unbelievable as that sounds I have to decline. This time," he added. "I'm quite happy where I am," he told her, thrusting into her a little more forcefully and causing her grip on his hair to tighten as a moan of pleasure escaped her.

"Not like that. I want to taste your..." Her voice trailed off as she raised her head and bit his shoulder.

"Are you sure?" His body stilled.

"That was what I wanted to tell you before you distracted me. Your surprise. I've thought about it a lot. I want to spend the rest of your life with you, not just the rest of mine. And hey, just because it isn't sexual doesn't mean it can't be. I want it to be...pleasant," she told him. "So I'll enjoy doing it. And I can't think of a more appealing time."

"If you're sure..."

"I am," she assured him.

Nodding, he allowed one of his fingernails to lengthen and used it to create a deep slash at the base of his neck, over his pulse.

As Willow lifted her head and began to drink from him, Seth thrust inside of her again. Both groaned deep in their throats as both her suckling and his thrusts became more forceful.

Unwilling to release his neck, even to scream with pleasure from her orgasm, Willow bit down instead. The action made him growl as he thrust into her then collapsed.

"Gods, is that what you feel?" he asked, his voice shaky.

Willow released his neck and kissed him, thrusting her tongue into his mouth. When the kiss ended she quickly licked his wound, watching in amazement as it closed before her eyes.

"It worked. Okay, that was cool," she told him almost distractedly, before she licked the trail of blood that had dripped down his chest.

When she finished, Seth leaned his head against her shoulder and chuckled. "I love you, Willow."

"Good, because I am completely in love with you. And just for the record, if I find you doing this biting thing with any other girl, you're dead meat faster than you can say 'all-you-can-eat-day-at-the-blood-bank'."

"Never, my love. You are the only woman I will ever want for the rest of my life."

"That's good to know. Now, show me how much you missed me," she told him, a mischievous twinkle in her eye.

"Isn't that what I've been doing?" he asked, playing along. "How much proof do you need? You were only away for two days this time..."

"No. That was just to ease the tension." Smiling, she pushed on his chest then climbed on top of him. "You, sir have created an insatiable need inside of me. Now, you must suffer the consequences."

Sighing deeply, he used his best martyred voice. "Well, if I must..." He knew his smile ruined the effect. "Or, you can show me just what you want." Lifting her to her knees, he guided her down onto his cock. "Show me the wild lover that hides deep inside of you."

Seth watched Willow's head fall backward, felt her hair tickling his thighs. Placing both hands on her hips, he tried to keep her movements slow.

Groaning, he knew he was in heaven when she lifted her hands to her own breasts. Cupping them, she teased him as she played with herself. His eyes were half-closed, as he enjoyed the show. One hand left her breast, resting behind her on his thigh. Above him, she arched her back, grinding against him as her golden hair fell between his legs. Long seconds later, he felt her nails scraping lightly against his balls. Her free hand moved to his and guided it to where they were joined.

Thrusting down, she guided his fingers to touch her, much as he had on their first night together.

"I love feeling you touch me," she moaned, her movements speeding up as his fingers plucked at her clit.

She released him, her hands moving to score his chest.

"Please don't ever stop touching me like this." She cried out, her muscles tightening around him. "God, Seth, don't stop."

Her contractions pulled an orgasm from him. Thrusting as deeply as possible given their position, he growled as he came.

"Ah, love, you do not know what you do to me," he whispered when he could speak again.

"Yes I do, because you have the same effect on me." Snuggling down onto his chest she sighed. "I've never felt safer than I do in your arms."

"I'm glad. You are truly a gift from the Moon Goddess to me."

"Moon Goddess?" Her voice was low, sleepy.

"Sleep, my love. I will tell you that story another night." Placing a tender kiss on her forehead, Seth pulled her hair back from her face when her breathing became even. Watching her sleep, he felt like the luckiest man in the world.

About the Author

To learn more about Sandy Lynn, please visit http://sandylynn.com. Send an email to Sandy at sandy@sandylynn.com or join her Yahoo! group to join in the fun with other readers as well as Sandy! http://groups.yahoo.com/group/Club_Strigoi

Look for these titles

Now Available

Night's Promise
Eye Candy

She's his target...and his mate. Aw, hell!

Carinian's Seeker
© *2007 TJ Michaels*

Beautiful genius Carinian Derrickson wants to live long enough to date a man from the future generations of spacemen, complete with ray guns and starships. She's not crazy, she's just afraid of dying young of some dreaded disease, like all the rest of her family. Her research into gene therapy has shown her the way to extend her life is by emulating traits only before seen in fiction. Vampire fiction. Only the beings that shouldn't exist are very real indeed.

Unknown to her, there's a bad boy vampire in the lab next door with a goal quite the opposite of hers. If he has his way, he'll bring the Vampire Council of Ethics (V.C.O.E.) to its knees.

Jon Bixler is a Seeker for the Council—an assassin and undercover operative in a world of humans. Bix must get close enough to this rogue to find out exactly how he plans to dismantle the Council. And Carinian is just the ticket. But when he meets her, all his vampire common sense flies out the window as his libido leaps off the charts. What's he going to do now that the woman is in danger and secretly trying to do the impossible?

Bix and Carin can't deny the combustion of love and lust between them. They accept their mating. But can they stay alive long enough to enjoy it?

Available now in ebook and print from Samhain Publishing.

Enjoy the following excerpt...

"Kiss me, Bix," she whispered fiercely, tilting her head up with eyes closed. She knew he'd give her what she asked for. No need to look. Just feel. Bix would take care of her. She felt his mouth move towards her, but he didn't meet her lips. Instead he tipped her chin up more and licked the side of her neck, from her pulse point up to her ear.

The intense answering ripple in her womb almost made her forget to erect a psychic shield.

"Oh damn, that was nasty. Do it again."

Bix gave her another hot swipe of his wet tongue along her sensitive skin. She shivered as her head fell back. Her skin felt much too tight and her body grew hotter by the second. She barely registered the crooning of the music in the background as she reached into his tailored jacket, grabbed two fists full of his shirt and held on under a sensual assault that almost bent her over backward. Moisture gathered at the entrance of her channel and even *she* could smell her arousal waft up from between her thighs. Finally, he captured her lips. Bix started growling again, but for a whole new set of reasons, all of which she agreed with wholeheartedly.

"I can smell you, baby. Makes me want to go down on my knees and bury my head under your dress right here in the middle of this dance floor."

Lord knows she wanted nothing more than to find a dark corner, flip up her skirt and let him have at it. A primal need rose up in her, a need for him to take her. To make her his in every way. Forever. Her kneecaps quivered and she spoke to them. *Don't you dare dump me on my ass. Stand firm, girl, stand firm.*

"Firm? I've got something firm for you, baby," Bix whispered into her head and pressed his long, swollen ridge of flesh firmly against her belly.

Her shield dropped like a stone. Bix, along with a horde of other horny vamps, heard her telepathic scream. *"Oh, Bix, I'm yours, baby. Please... Oh God, bite me."*

He looked directly into her eyes, fangs clearly visible. "Are you sure, Carin? There's no going back if we do this."

She rubbed feverishly against him, trying to do her best to look like she was still dancing rather than humping against his leg. "Yes, I'm sure, Bix. I'm yours, and you're mine. I can't imagine being with anyone else or sharing you with anyone else. Ever."

"The mating is to bind you to me, not the other way around," Bix said firmly, all smug Seeker confidence.

Alpha to the bone, arrogant and self-assured. And right now, she didn't give a rat's ass. "So you say, damn it. You're mine."

She knew she could be a stubborn bitch on wheels, but this man was going to be wholly and completely hers and love it. Even if she had to kill him. Her breathing hitched with anticipation as he lowered his head to the sweet pulse on her neck. She could feel his fangs aching fiercely, his need to bite so strong, *her* gums tingled. So powerful it burned from where his mouth touched her down to the little hairs on her toes. He rubbed his incisors against her tender skin.

A sharp voice cut through the fog of lust and need.

"Bix and Carin, please join me on the dais." Alaana Serati stood there, calling to them. "And no necking on the dance floor for you two. We will do this according to tradition." Then she smiled at Bix's grimace at having his love play interrupted.

"Damn, her timing sucks," Carin growled into his chest.

GET IT NOW

MyBookStoreAndMore.com

GREAT EBOOKS, GREAT DEALS . . . AND MORE!

Don't wait to run to the bookstore down the street, or
waste time shopping online at one of the "big boys." Now,
all your favorite Samhain authors are all in one place—at
MyBookStoreAndMore.com. Stop by today and discover
great deals on Samhain—and a whole lot more!

Samhain
Publishing, Ltd.

WWW.SAMHAINPUBLISHING.COM

FLY AWAY

Discover the Talons Series

5 STEAMY NEW PARANORMAL ROMANCES
TO HOOK YOU IN

Kiss Me Deadly, by Shannon Stacey
King of Prey, by Mandy M. Roth
Firebird, by Jaycee Clark
Caged Desire, by Sydney Somers
Seize the Hunter, by Michelle M. Pillow

AVAILABLE IN EBOOK—COMING SOON IN PRINT!

WWW.SAMHAINPUBLISHING.COM

Printed in the United Kingdom
by Lightning Source UK Ltd.
135236UK00001B/285/A